Sarah

The study that Sarah Marsden sat in was a shadow of its former glory. First built in the early 1900's it was the height of decadence at the time. Mahogany panelling, a single wingback chair pointed at the fireplace. It was a room to retreat to as opposed to work in. A testament to the perceived greatness of the man for who it was built. Sarah's in-law, Giles' great grandfather; Thomas Marsden.

Although she had never met the man she had heard the same stories about him time and time again. When she and Giles had first started dating Giles' mother had often used the dinner table as a podium to espouse the achievements of her grandfather. How he single handedly built his empire through hard work and an uncanny business acumen. The subtext of the tiresome monologues was that they were better. Better than most, but definitely better than Sarah. The pride in her future mother in laws voice was hollow, characteristic of the life she had led. Void of personal achievement, void of dreams. Only the bitterness she held so close kept her human.

Sarah would hide a knowing smirk behind her crystal wine glass when Giles rolled his eyes and mocked his mother when she wasn't looking. Back then he had a joie de vivre fuelled by adolesence and money. He was intoxicating. He was the anthesis of the life she had known. Even now Sarah couldn't help but smile when she thought about the man he was when they had first met.

Those days felt as far away as the days of Thomas Marsden himself. The responsibilities of adulthood had chipped away at both of them. Or maybe it was just adulthood was exposing the cracks that had always been there. Cracks that were covered by the flush of love in its infancy. This thought had become more and more persistent in the last year. It now floated in her head pulling at memories with a clarity that only time can bring. She wondered why Giles had waited until his mother had passed away before they got married. It was no secret that her prospective mother in law did not like Sarah. But that didn't matter to Giles, at least that's what he'd said at the time. So why did he wait? Sarah had moved into the mansion the day after the funeral, they married a month later and Poppy arrived that November. It happened so fast after waiting for so long. At the time Sarah was happy, happy they were moving forward. Looking back, Giles had been waiting until his mother passed away before they did anything because he would never get her approval.

Heavy raindrops spattered loudly against the single pane windows as they released their weight pulling Sarah back to the present, although that was hard to do. Visual reminders of the generations that occupied the mansion before her were everywhere she looked. Layers of nicotine stained paint peeled from the corners of the walls. Her chair stood on a faded rug that had

To Protect

DEDICATION

To Lou, you believed before me.

CHAPTERS

Whenever people speak of the capacity of man to change they eulogise the teachings of mother nature. Winter turning to Spring. The butterfly breaking free of its chrysalis. That change itself is powerful and positive.

It is also true that when a snake sheds its skin it remains a snake.

more dust than thread. She had wanted to throw it out years ago but Giles and her had argued. It had been bought by Giles' grandmother and he demanded it stayed. It was his family's home, she wouldn't understand. She didn't have heirlooms. He was right, she didn't understand. She couldn't.

It wasn't just the rug though. Sarah had wanted to make changes to the mansion, to make it feel like their home. Nesting in anticipation of Poppy. But Giles had said he wasn't ready. It was too soon after his mother's death. She had respected that. But now? Poppy is almost nine and she still isn't allowed to decorate. Each thought pulled at another. They came readily. Well trodden mental paths, each knew where it needed to go to confirm a theory. Sarah had found herself becoming lost in these thoughts most days and nights recently. How symbols of a by-gone era owned by others, not her, infected her life. Relatives that she had never met literally hung over her, she passed their oil painted portraits in the hall daily. She could feel their presence, the ghosts of former family glories. Ghosts that gripped her soul.

She was in the study to go through her now nightly ritual of sifting through the pile of bills that had accumulated and weeding out what she could avoid paying. She had split the paperwork into two piles; 'can still wait' and 'immediate payment.' The immediate payment pile had been getting bigger every week and Sarah's ability to juggle finances was no longer enough.

She stared down at the green leather writing surface of the desk, scored and cracked from holding the secrets it took to build the linen empire. She wondered what secrets it held. Could it take hers? Allow her to release her burdens into its silence. She couldn't. She wasn't ready to face the things she had done. The things she still had to do. A tear fell from her cheek onto a final reminder.

She stood from the desk and went to the rain lashed window overlooking the courtyard. Lost in thought she pulled at her wedding ring. It had loosened over the last few months as the stress had begun to take its toll. She was losing more weight than she wanted to, her knuckle was barely keeping the ring on her finger. Her secrets had become too great. No-one must know about them. No-one can know about the young girl she kept locked in a cell. She'll free her tomorrow, but into something much worse.

At the border

The wipers rubbed across the windscreen simultaneously clearing the raindrops and sharpening the headlights of the oncoming traffic. Although it wasn't night time yet the darkness of the clouds made it seem later than it was, making visibility poor and headlights essential. This was normal in Ireland no matter the time of year, but especially in October.

'Is there any coffee left?' Remi Wallace, the driver asked as another lorry shook the car on its way past.

'A dribble, but it's gone cold now, you want it?' Sam answered from the back.

'Nah, you're alright, I'll let you have it'

They had been cooped up inside the unmarked mondeo for over three hours on the verge of the A1 just before the border between Northern Ireland and the Republic of Ireland and the chat had gone as stale as the coffee.

'Are we sure this guy is even going to show?' Sam asked no-one in particular. The youngest of the team by almost a decade he fitted in nicely. He was like a younger brother, it suited him, and the rest of the team.

'He's going to show, we just don't know where. The boat docked in Greenore just over an hour ago. If we get lucky we'll pick him up when he drives past. In the meantime I have the pleasure of listening to your incessant crap.' Louise gave a wry smile in the mirror catching Sam's eye. She was the team leader, not just in title but in reality. This was her team, she'd hand picked the other three. As with everything Louise did she'd done her homework. It had paid off, they were a good team. Every now and then she had to slap an ego down but that was a small price to pay for going home happy each night and giving her kids a cuddle. These three guys helped her marriage, she knew it and so did Tom and the kids. They were part of her family. She loved them all, but Remi was her favourite, no doubt.

As normal he drove the car, mostly because of his frame, at 6'4" and just under 20 stone the car was a happier place when he was in the front. He was the first that she'd asked to join the team two years ago. At the time he had had a public complaint against him for excessive force. Ultimately he was cleared, it just so happens at his size any amount of force is deemed excessive. The investigation had got to him though and he was looking for a change. Louise's timing was perfect. At the time he was pure muscle, now his wife was pregnant and he'd gained a few pounds of sympathy. In truth, more than a few pounds but Louise was sure no-one wanted to find out whether he still had the power or not.

'Look lively people. White van approaching.' Remi broke the silence. 'Registration plate XAZ 7876 , that our guy?'

'That's him' Ben confirmed from the back seat.

'Unit 3 to command, we have visual. Moving in.' Louise threw the radio on the dashboard as Remi edged the car forward to get a clearing in the traffic. As the van went passed the driver shot a sideways glance, he caught their eyes. All four in the car could see the colour drain from his cheeks instantly. He was caught and he knew it, now it was just a matter of whether he accepted it or not.

Remi floored the mondeo to catch up, the lights behind the front grill flashing as traffic moved to the inner lane. Within minutes he was behind the van. He pulled into the outer lane alongside and Louise rolled down the window. She used her gun to indicate to the driver to pull over. The driver's face calculated his chances and for a split second Remi hoped he was going to get to stretch the car for a bit, but then the van slowed and the driver pulled over to the hard shoulder. Remi pulled up behind him while Louise reported to command, they'd be here soon enough.

'You stay here boss, we'll check him out'

'And miss out on the fun stuff, no chance.' Louise was already out of the car as she shot her response. 'Sam, you take the back door, Ben you divert traffic to the outside lane while Remi & I have a chat with the driver. Remi you take him, I'll take passenger side'

'Yes Boss.' All three harmonised.

The rain had subsided to a heavy drizzle as both Remi and Louise walked the length of the van, its diesel engine clattering on idle. Ben had his torch from his side and was signalling for traffic to stay to the right of the carriageway.

As he approached the drivers' door Remi unlatched his gun just in case. He saw the window was rolled down already. He took a wider arc as he approached the driver's window keeping himself out of reach.

The bark and snarl of the drivers' dog made him step back even further out of reach as the dog almost leapt out of the window, teeth showing, barking ferociously, only his body jamming in the gap kept him in the van.

'Dog! Dog!' Remi screamed, louder than he'd hoped he would. 'Get the fucking pole!'

'What?' Sam poked his head round from the back of the van

'Keep that thing in the van or I'll shoot it!' Remi directed the driver. 'The pole, get the pole now!' It was Sam who was now receiving a mouthful from Remi.

Sam went to the car and starting running back to Remi with the dog pole in hand. 'Don't give it to me! Get the dog, I'll keep an eye on the driver'

'Roll the fucking window up now. And get that dog under control' Remi was barking orders to everyone at the same time.

Remi's reaction gave the driver a false sense of bravado, and he began laughing at Remi from under his baseball cap. 'Yeah, get him Tyson, get him. The pig bastard!'

Sam tried to loop the leash around the neck of the dog while it was poking out of the window but the driver was taunting him by moving Tyson's body this way and that to keep him from hooking the dog. The driver pulled the dog in to the cab of the van completely and stuck his head out and began to mock Remi and Sam with fake barking noises. Remi got more pissed off by this and grabbed the handle of the door 'ok, you wee bastard c'mere' but as he did the drivers' head was replaced by Tyson's drooling mouth and genuine deafening barks. Remi jumped back from the door, this

time making no excuses for his fear of dogs.   He'd
hated them ever since his brother had been mauled by a
neighbours dog when they were younger. Anyone who
ever told him dogs were harmless he only had to show
the scar running from forehead to chin across his
brother's face. Some might be harmless but he wasn't
taking the chance.

'Playtime's over.' Louise held the gun to the back of
the head of the driver. She'd opened the passenger door
while he was entertaining himself scaring the crap out
of Remi. 'Let my officer take your dog and step out of
the car.'

'Piss off, you won't shoot me'

'Fair point.' She pulled her police issue Glock 17
pistol away from his neck but kept it pointed at him
from a distance. 'But I will shoot your dog.' Louise
moved the gun in the direction of Tyson who was still
barking out the window. 'It's pretty easy, a dangerous
dog like that, Bullmastiff if I'm correct?'

'Yeah'. The driver put a protective arm around his
pet.

'See I'm more of a cat person myself.' Louise
continued 'Let my officer take control of the dog and
he'll be fine. Continue to play about and I'll shoot
him.'

It didn't take long for the point to sink in. 'Alright,
alright. Take it easy with Tyson' The driver opened the
door and held Tyson while Sam looped the noose
around its neck. The driver was in his early twenties,
his frame as underdeveloped as the moustache that
tickled his upper lip. He stepped out of the van and was
met by Remi who threw him up against the side of the
van with just one hand. 'That dog comes anywhere

near me again and I'll slice its throat' came the whisper in the young mans ear. The driver's bravado from earlier instantly left him. He had no reason to doubt the sincerity behind the message.

'Have you any more dogs in the back of this van? If I open this, nothing is going to jump out and attack me is it?' Louise shouted over at the driver from the backdoor.

Trying to hold on to what little remained of his manliness the driver shot back 'Six lions and twelve tig-' he didn't finish the response before his head bounced off the side panelling making raindrops flee while leaving a small dent.

Louise opened the back doors of the van, it was as they had expected. They had received a tip off earlier detailing as much. The back of the van held at least a dozen blue barrels with the distinct smell of diesel emanating from them. Sam and Louise climbed into the back of the van and had a look around.

'Boss, have a look here' Sam was shining his torch behind one line of barrels. 'He must have a lot of cats!' There was at least ten 30 litre bags of cat litter stuffed up against the wall of the van.

'If I didn't know any better, I'd suggest you were using the cat litter to extract the dye from the fuel'. Louise calmly spoke in the direction of the driver. 'Stupid prick.' She genuinely felt for him, he'd thrown his life away for a couple of hundred quid. 'Alright, we have enough to keep him. Keep looking around the van while I go and arrest him'

'Sure thing boss. You want me to dip the diesel?'

'Nah, we'll take the van back and do it where it'll be warmer. I'll put a steak dinner for all of you on it that its red.'

Sam smiled, that was one dinner he wouldn't be getting.

Louise jumped back on to the tarmac and nodded to Remi to put him under arrest.

An hour later a squad car had taken the driver away and Tyson was on his was to the police kennels as the squad were waiting for the tow truck to take the van back to the station.

'Anyone fancy a smoke?' Sam offered up a couple of boxes of cigarettes he found in the drivers glove box.

'Where are they from?' Ben asked, relieved to be off traffic directing duty.

'Dunno, Russia maybe? Looks Russian going by the writing, I'm not great on my languages but I found a bottle that smelt like vodka in the drivers door so I'm guessing Russian'

'No label on the vodka?'

'None. I'll grab it.' Sam went to the drivers door and pulled out a glass bottle and passed it round the group. 'Have a sniff, definitely vodka'

Each one of them reacted as though smelling milk that was a couple of days passed its sell by date.

'Any of you seen or smelt anything like this before?' Louise asked as she held the bottle away from her.

'Maybe when I was a student back at some random house party, but nothing I remember. I'm an old man now, a few Guinness on a night off is as far as I stretch these days, give it to the party animal to check' Remi laughed.

'I'll have a taste and see. Vodka is a speciality of mine.' Sam took a swig from the bottle. Acting like a true connoisseur he let the drink settle in his mouth and then swallowed. For a second there was no reaction. Then it came. 'Ack, ack' swiftly followed by wheezing and coughing. 'What the fuck?'

'Not good then?' Ben laughed at his colleague.

'Ah to be young' Remi slapped Sam on the back to help clear his throat.

'That's a home brew. A strong one at that. Whoever is brewing this shit likes their vodka.'

We meet Tatyana

Wind whistled through the gaps of the stone walls slowly calling to life a cold that had settled deep in Tatyana's bones over the last few days when the cell she now lay in had become her home. She wasn't sure how long it had been since she was first thrown here or why. What she did know was that she was being watched. She pulled the blanket that she'd been left with around her shoulders and looked for answers in the darkness that had been her only companion as the blanket settled on her skin like the regret of a lost love.

Her cell was pitch black with three items in it, none of which she owned. A thin mattress that was too small to fully stretch out on so she had to curl up awkwardly if she wanted all of her slender 5'4" frame to stay off the floor which brought new definition to the term stone cold. A steel bucket that was replaced regularly if she needed to take care of any business, and the blanket she had now removed from her shoulders as the penance of its meagre warmth was an itch that tried to burrow through her skin. Unlike the bucket the blanket hadn't been replaced and smelt as badly as her clothes which were the same ones that she had left her home filled with hope of a new life wearing.

Her hands and knuckles had slowly started to heal and skin was beginning to reform where it had blistered or shredded from hitting the walls and door in frustration and anger when she was first thrown in here.

After initially resisting she had stopped fighting her prison and started to feel it, embrace it. Her eyes were slowly adjusting to her surroundings. She couldn't see, yet. Darkness was all she could make out but she was learning to understand the gradients of blackness. She memorised where the door was after they changed her bucket a couple of meals ago but since then they've moved her mattress and bucket every time someone comes into the room keeping her disorientated. She has to start from scratch every time relearning. It helps pass the time. They don't know this has helped her. Instead of learning one small part she is going to learn it all. Soon she will know the room better than herself, the shadows will become her friends.

She had presumed it was sex straight away and waited for it to come every time the huge steel door unlocked. She'd prepared for the rape mentally so she could get through it. If she didn't resist it wouldn't be as violent, unless that was their thing anyway. For the first couple of days she'd half heartedly laughed at the prospect. How many miles had she travelled to get away from her brothers and their friends to find herself somewhere worse? But it wasn't sex, it never came. Not yet anyway. At least at home she had some elements of control, here she had none. In her fifteen years of life she'd thought she'd learnt to understand the rules of the game but now the rules had changed and no-one told her.

Did Sarah betray her? *No.* She couldn't have. She

was so kind and understanding, she didn't judge. Maybe Sarah was looking for her right now? No, she wasn't. She couldn't think like that, *"you're on your own, again."* Internally Tatyana scolded herself for such weak thinking. No-one cared she was here, and no-one knew she was here. Apart from the guard who didn't speak. Occasionally he would give her a luke-warm bowl of soup and some water, she wasn't sure if was once a day or twice a day. She had lost any ability to track time. She didn't sleep anymore, instead she drifted in and out of various states of awareness. When she asked a question the only response she got was her own echo on the damp walls. A couple of meals ago, she had felt her way along the darkness to the side of the door and waited for him to come with the food. The door was steel and heavy so she could hear him unlocking it before he came in. She waited. As he came into the room she pushed him forward and ran through the doorway. Her chance at freedom. She ran forward ignoring the door, leaving it open. She ran as fast as she could. She ran straight into another guard who wrapped her up in strong muscled arms and placed her back onto the thin mattress in the corner. Again no one spoke. Or maybe they did and her screams drowned them out.

She wasn't sure what was worse, being raped every night by the people you knew or being left alone in the dark by people you didn't. As a tear trickled down her cheek she slowly felt herself beginning to crumble from the inside out.

An empty home

Remi gently put the key into the lock and squeezed the handle of the front door. He was later than he'd thought he'd be. The tow truck hadn't shown up and they had to arrange another one. He was frozen from the inside out and needed a long hot shower. He cursed himself as the door creaked reminding him to oil the hinges in the same way it had done for the last eight months. He threw his kit bag in its usual place at the front door and moved into the kitchen. There was no sign of Laura. As he suspected she'd be sleeping, at least tonight she'd made it to bed. She had been making a habit of falling asleep on the sofa over the last couple of weeks. He went to the fridge to get a beer before disturbing her. Held up behind the bottle opener magnet was a note. 'Can't sleep, bump is restless gone for a walk. Will call in with Jane. Dinner in the pot, just needs heated. She's excited to meet you, she's been kicking all day. Love you xx'.

A night to himself. A cold beer and dinner already made. This was an unexpected surprise. He scooped a bowl of stew out of the pot and stuck it in the microwave for three minutes while he checked the TV for something he could watch. Nights like these were going to become few and far between in the future. At thirty-five years old he was ready for a family. He always felt sorry for guys who had settled down earlier when he talked to them. He could hear the regret in their voices, the regret for what they thought they'd missed out on.

The microwave pinged and he grabbed another beer from the fridge kicking it closed with his foot as he went to settle into the sofa for an hour of peace and quiet. As he set his dinner on the coffee table there was a catalogue open with a post it 'what you think??' placed over a picture of a buggy or transportation system or what ever the hell the marketeers were calling it these days. He smiled, she knew him well. The buggy was nice, as far as buggies go but at least he'd be able to take the wee one outside on some trails with it. He'd met Laura six years earlier and they'd fallen in love straight away, despite how much she protested they didn't. Life moved pretty quickly for them and they'd bought their house a year later. They hadn't stretched themselves as they both wanted a family and felt being at home was more important than being in the office paying off a mortgage. There were pros and cons of doing things this way. The pros were now shortly going to show themselves as Laura would be able to take a full year maternity without impacting them greatly. They would be broke but they could survive. The cons, well, Remi was getting more and more experience of DIY than he ever wanted, the house definitely needed work.

His body ached as he lay back into the sofa. The last few days had been harder than he thought. He took another swig from his beer and rested his eyes as the

TV showed highlights of last nights football.

Tatyana huddled into her blanket. She pulled her knees closer to her chest, that way she would be able to wrap the sheet around her feet at least for a short while. How had she let herself get like this? She envied the girls she saw on TV and in posters. They never spoke with sadness. She missed her gran, she missed the way she brushed her hair and sang to her and cooked for her. If only gran was alive to see her now, she'd help. *No. Gran couldn't see her, no way, not like this.* Tatyana couldn't remember the last time she saw her reflection but she was sure it wasn't good. Her blonde hair would be dirty and her eyes puffed from crying. No, gran could never see her like this. She had to be stronger than this for her. She sat up and told herself she had to be stronger. She sat on the mattress hugging her knees teaching herself, talking to herself. *You're cold, you're tired and you're hungry, but you're safe. So far. No-one has tried to hurt you, you can get through this. You've suffered worse.* She stood up and went to her bucket to pee. They'd moved the bucket. Again. She began to search for the bucket on her hands and knees groping in the dark for something, hoping it was steel and not furry, or alive. After a minute of hopelessness her right fingertip brushed alongside the bucket. She inched forward and grabbed it, the coldness almost comforting. As she squatted in the darkness it hit her that her body might not be violated in this place but her mind, her only sanctuary, the only place that could be hers and hers alone for the last nine years has been taken from her. Whatever strength she had left in her legs evaporated and she collapsed on the floor knocking the bucket and contents over her leg as she sobbed alone in the darkness.

Remi woke having spilt the remains of his beer over his jeans. 'Shit!' He checked his watch as he rubbed his jeans with his sleeve to no avail. It was almost one am. It was unlike Laura to not wake him when she got in. He picked up his dishes and put the unopened beer back in the fridge.   Something didn't feel right though. There was no sign of Laura in the house at all. Normally her boots and coat would be lying somewhere. He went upstairs to see if she was in bed and had left them there. The bed was untouched from this morning.   She wasn't in the spare room either. Remi checked every room in the house but she wasn't anywhere. Outside, her car was in the driveway as it was when he'd come home. He got his phone from his kit bag at the door.   There were no missed calls. Strange. He phoned her mobile. It started to vibrate on the kitchen table. 'For fuck sake, what's the point of a mobile phone'. He hung up his own phone and picked up Laura's. One missed call. His. Of course. No other calls or text messages. This was definitely strange. It was now just after one am.   Far too late to phone anyone. This isn't normal though. He dialled Jane's number and let it ring. It went to voicemail and he left a message asking her to call him on Laura's phone as soon as she gets the message. Half an hour ago he could have slept for a week, now there was no chance of him sleeping.   He went back to his dishes and washed them as well as two mugs and side plates that Laura had left from earlier. There was no hot water so he boiled the kettle to pass some more time.   He finished washing the six items and checked both phones in case he'd missed a call or text while he was washing. He hadn't. The clock had moved forward four minutes though. Nerves started to build inside him. *What has happened? Has she had to go to hospital? They would have phoned. They have his number, don't they?*

He opened a drawer and pulled out a clean towel to dry the six items with. *That should be enough time passed to warrant another phonecall.* Both mugs were now placed in the cupboard and the clock on his phone had moved forward another two minutes. He dialled Jane's number again and left another voicemail. He had a quick glance through her text messages but there was nothing unusual. He dialled Jane's number a third time. This time he wouldn't leave a voicemail, there was nothing else to say. At least she could see the amount of missed calls and know it was urgent. He hung up as it went to voicemail. *What now?*

He flicked through the contacts in Laura's phone and saw 'Jane home'. He called this number incase her mobile was on silent. This time it didn't go to voicemail but after fourteen rings he hung up. He tried Jane's mobile one last time.

'Hello?' the woman's voice at the other end had clearly just woken up.

'Jane?'

'Who's this?'

'Jane, it's me Remi, Laura's husband'

'Remi? Did you just call the house?'

'Yes, I did, I'm sorry. Was Laura with you tonight?'

'Laura? Yes. She left ages ago. Is she alright?' there was an alertness to Jane's voice now as her brain was catching up with her speech.

'I dunno, she hasn't come home. What time did she leave yours at?'

'Hold on' Remi could hear a bedside light being flicked on and the involuntary noise you make when your eyes are exposed to light too quickly from the other end of the line. 'She stayed later than normal, but she must have left about an hour ago now.'

'Shit. Did she get a taxi?'

'No. She wanted to walk, she was hoping to tire herself out as the baby was restless and she didn't fancy another night of no sleep'

'OK. If she calls can you phone me on her phone. I'll have it with me.'

'Is everything ok?'

'I'm not sure, I'll let you know.'

Sarah to the rescue

Muffled voices in the distance woke Tatyana up from her depression induced sleep. It took her a few seconds to register what the noises were. As soon as she did she dismissed her tiredness, her cold and stood to her feet. Her jeans were still round her ankles from when she fell over as she yelled at the top of her voice. She went to the walls and reopened the cuts on her hands by banging on the stone as she tried to find the door. Her screams came to no avail, for ten minutes she stood at the door, her voice becoming hoarser and hoarser refusing to break into a sob. If there was any light she would have seen her blood staining the steel of the door. Eventually the adrenaline left her and her energy drained away again and she collapsed at the foot of the door too weak to stand. The sobs that she'd been holding back came freely now.

Tatyana hadn't moved from the foot of the door when she heard the outside lock being moved. She crawled away from the door through her own urine that was still lying on the floor and curled up at a wall away from the door. She checked with her hands there was nothing around her. They didn't have to touch her. They would leave a bowl at her feet as normal and leave. *Please leave.* The second lock was released. One more to go. She quickly pulled her wet jeans up incase she was inviting them to have their way.

Every other time they came into the room she had tried to face them, either standing or sitting she would look to where she thought they were. This time she stayed hugging her knees and faced sideways to the door. She couldn't do this anymore. They had broken her. Her spirit had finally left.

As the third lock was released she saw a shard of light and heard voices. They were louder. They were male. She readied herself. She knew what was coming. Again she caressed the floor hoping to find something to use as a weapon, a nail, a stone, anything. Inside she cursed herself for being so weak. She was prepared earlier but they had broken her. Now she was about to pay. The adrenaline started to pump through her veins again, her breathing became more deliberate as she raced to control it. She changed her body position from submissive along the wall to poised for attack. She wouldn't resist one man, but if they tried to rape her together she would fight them all.

'Everyone wait here' a female voice from behind the door commanded. 'Give me the torch. The poor girl must be terrified.' The door opened further and the torch light shone on the floor. Although it was a weak torch it almost blinded Tatyana.

'Tatyana?' The voice came from behind the door 'Tatyana, it's Sarah Marsden. I met you back in Belarus. I'm coming inside alone, is that ok?'

Tatyana could barely respond as her fear turned to relief in an instant. She didn't have to fight anymore. Tatyana fell back against the wall. Her tears this time were a mixture of joy, relief and embarrassment.

Sarah slowly entered the room and saw that Tatyana was shying away from the light even though it was pointed at the ground. 'Tatyana, sweetie, it's Sarah. I've come to get you. I'm so sorry it took me so long to find you. I have some friends with me outside. I'm going to ask them to put their torches on so there is some light while I talk to you. Then I'm going to turn my torch off and bring you some warm soup, a blanket and some fresh clothes. The clothes might be a little big but they are clean. Is that ok?' Tatyana remained silent at the back of the room. Sarah nodded to her colleagues behind the door and the light shifted from outside the room to inside.

'Tatyana, I'm coming in with a blanket and some soup first.' Sarah opened the door further and she could see Tatyana huddled against the wall. When she reached her she spoke even more softly.

'I'm here sweetie, I'm here. I'm so so sorry we lost you. You're safe now.' She stroked Tatyana's hair as she talked her through everything she was doing.

'I have a clean blanket here for you, I'm just going to wrap it round your shoulders.' Tatyana allowed her to lay the blanket across her back.

'I'm sorry' Tatyana could barely muster the words together.

'Ssssshhhhh, you don't have to say anything. You're safe. Let me look after you. When you're out of here and if you want to talk I'll listen. You don't have to say anything now. OK?'

Tatyana turned to face her and nodded. Although Sarah could barely see in front of her Tatyana could see clearly as though it was the middle of the day. Sarah's face, long and slim.   Her hair was tied back in a ponytail this time.   Her eyes weren't as kind as she remembered but that was maybe because Tatyana had let her down.

'Here's some soup, I made it myself so it's not that good but it's warm. We'll get you something proper to eat when we get you home.'   Sarah poured a bowl of soup from a flask and put her arm around Tatyana and held her closely until she had finished. Neither of them said anything.

After the soup was finished Sarah took the bowl and set it on the ground.

'Do you think you'd be ready to leave now?'

Tatyana nodded her head.

'OK.   I have some clean clothes.   I'll bring them in and then give you some privacy to change.   I'll be outside the door.'

'Don't leave' Tatyana panicked and gripped Sarah's jacket.

'I'm not leaving. I'll be right here sweetie.'

'Don't leave' was all Tatyana could say. 'Please'

'I'm not leaving. I promise. I'm here. I'll stay here. I'll get the guys to hand me the clothes and then close the door over so you can change.' As Sarah stood up Tatyana instinctively grabbed her arm.

'It's OK sweetie.   It's OK. I'm going nowhere' Tatyana reluctantly let go of her arm.

'Peter?' Sarah spoke to her team outside. 'Can you pass me the clothes and pull the door closed a little more but don't shut it'

A bundle of clean clothes were passed through the gap in the door and once Sarah had them in her hands the door was pulled so only the smallest sliver of light could be seen.

'OK sweetie, here's some clothes for you. I'm sorry they aren't that nice and they probably don't fit but they are clean. Take your time and don't worry, we'll gather up your own clothes and get them washed for you when we get home.'

Tatyana pulled on the tracksuit bottoms, clean t-shirt and hoody. Sarah was right, they didn't fit but they were clean and they felt so good against her skin.

'Are they ok?'

'Yes, thank you. I'm so sorry'

'Please, stop saying sorry, you have nothing to say sorry for. I'm sorry that it took us so long to find you. Alright. You have absolutely nothing to be sorry for. OK?'

'OK.'

'You think you're ready to leave?'

'Yeah'

'Good. Because I'm ready to take you home. There is one thing that I have to do, I don't want to do it but we have to. I'm going to tell you what it is so you don't worry. You have to trust me, OK?'

'I do.'

'Good. I don't know if you know or not but it is the middle of the day outside and it is for once a very bright day. Now I don't know how long you've been in here for but we lost track of you eight days ago. That means you most likely have been here for a week in complete darkness. Your eyes won't be ready for the sun yet, or the lights just outside this room if we turn them on. If we don't protect your eyes we could do you more damage. Do you understand?'

'Yes'

'Good. I hope you don't mind and I hope you trust me because I'm only going to do this to help. Outside we have a hood that will blackout all light. I'm going to put it over your head until we get you home. Once we get you home we can get you adjusted to normal light when you are ready. My house is over a three hours drive away, but I'll be in the backseat beside you the whole way. You can hold my hand if you want.'

'OK. Please don't leave me.'

'I won't. Take my hand and don't let go until you want to.' Tatyana slipped her hand into Sarah's and gripped tighter than Sarah had expected her to.

'It's all over now sweetie, time to go to your new home.' Sarah spoke softly as she gently pulled the hood over Tatyana's head.

Broken car, broken wife

The blue lights were flashing in the distance and Remi's heart began to race. His mind began fighting with itself. His instant thoughts were Laura had been hurt, the blue flashes were intermittently lighting her face as she lay on a pavement. This dialogue was overwhelming his rational side which was failing in its argument that the lights were someone else's misfortune. As he rounded the corner the scene didn't alleviate any fears. There were three police cars and an ambulance blocking the most of the country road. In behind he could see a land rover had mounted the pavement and crashed into a streetlight.

He pulled his car over to the side and got out. The rain from earlier had eased off but it was bitterly cold with a north wind cutting across the faces of the officers standing at the perimeter so Remi zipped his jacket up fully as he went to get any information he could. The officer who was posted in front was a few years his junior. Remi recognised his face but couldn't remember his name.

'Hey' Remi nodded as he approached. He could see the officer knew his face but couldn't picture where from. 'I'm Remi. OCTF' He could see the officer twig.

'Dan. It's a pretty nasty accident'

'Dan. My wife hasn't come home, is there a woman involved?' Remi asked looking past the officer. He did't need an answer as he saw Laura being lifted on to a stretcher by the ambulance crew. It didn't matter that her face was mostly covered by an oxygen mask, he recognised her instantly. Remi was at her side in an instant before Dan could stop him.

'Is she alright?' he asked no-one in particular.

'Too early to tell' one of the ambulance crew answered as she was lifted into the back of the ambulance.

'I'm her husband. Where are you taking her?'

'The Ulster. You can see her there. I'm sorry.' The crew member jumped into the back of the ambulance beside Laura and shut the door. A few seconds later the ambulance was on its way leaving Remi standing at the side of the road on his own.

He wasn't alone for too long as Dan approached with his superior. An older man called Stephen. Remi knew him from before he transferred to the task force. They didn't see eye to eye on most things in life and mostly tried to keep their distance until one night they had all went out for a few drinks. Words were said and punches thrown. Two of Stephen's team ended up in hospital that night. Remi didn't.

'Remi. Dan here tells me that was your wife? I'm sorry.'

'What happened Steve? Will she be ok?'

'As far as we can tell the driver of the Land Rover was coming home, pulled out of the side road there. Judging by the tyre marks it looks as though it was drifting to the other side of the road and either something made him correct, possibly an oncoming car, but there are no other marks and you'd hope that someone would stop if they saw this in their rear view mirror. More probably he realised he was drifting and over corrected.'

'Drunk?'

'He's over the limit, but he's asked for a blood test to confirm so he's being taken to the station now.' Remi ran to the police car where the driver of the Land Rover was sitting in the back seat.

'Stop him!' Stephen yelled, but Dan was already a step ahead. He had caught up with Remi and was holding him back as much as he could. 'Take it easy big man. You don't want do anything stupid. This guy is scum, you lay one finger on him and he'll sue you before the bruise healed. He's not worth it.' Dan stood between Remi and the police car physically pushing him back with both arms blocking his path.

'Get that fucker down to the station — now!' Stephen commanded his officers. It was only when the constable jumped into the front seat and started the engine that Dan let go of Remi. The police car pulled started to slowly exit the scene. As it did Remi stood still and followed the man in the back seat with his stare. As the police car slowly negotiated the other cars and bollards the driver of the Land Rover looked only at the headrest in front of him. It was only when the constable had found a path and was about to accelerate away did the man in the backseat turn to face Remi, give him a smile and wave.

'Who the fuck is that prick?' Remi shouted after the police car.

'That prick is Giles Marsden. He owns Marsden house.'

'Never heard of him, or it. Just make sure you get him. I have to go and look after my family.'

A new start for Tatyana

Tatyana lay her head on Sarah's shoulder and slept for most of the way in the car, her body ached from lack of sleep and cold. She didn't mind having the hood over her head, it helped her sleep. She could feel Sarah's presence the whole time, her arm gently resting on her leg comforting her. Tatyana felt a gentle tapping on her shoulder and Sarah whispered to her that they were almost home.

'I'm going to take the hood off now sweetie, ok? The daylight has almost faded now and we're nearly home'

Tatyana sat up and waited for her hood to be taken off. 'Keep your eyes closed as I pull up' Sarah reminded her.

Tatyana squeezed her eyes closed in anticipation of the light burning her retinas. As the hood was removed she could feel the intense light filtering through her eyelids.

'Keep your eyes closed for another couple of minutes' Sarah asked her. Tatyana sat in the back seat of the car with her eyes closed trying to make out every sound, every corner the car took. The road was no longer smooth, it hadn't been for some time, she'd felt the change even in her sleep. She had become accustomed to the light filtering through her eyelids and slowly opened them. She managed to keep them open for a split second before automatically shutting the light out again. After five or six long slow blinks Tatyana had her eyes open as she looked out the window of the Range Rover. She didn't know much about cars, but she knew it wasn't new, that didn't matter to Tatyana, it was warm and it was safe.

Although there were no street lights and the moon wasn't particularly bright that evening Tatyana could see everything around her. The trees stood so tall and proud as they towered over the stone wall that flanked the road. Tatyana imagined that the wall was the outer perimeter of a country manor and she was being whisked away to live there. In the morning she would get up and feed her horses, then take them for a walk through the forest breaking into a gallop as the trees cleared and the fields opened in front of her. She would kick harder and the horse would run faster, her heart racing with joy as she was taken further and further away from her troubles. She wouldn't look back, there was no need to. She would only look ahead, into the brightness.

The driver turned the car into a driveway and Sarah whispered 'We're home' but Tatyana couldn't see a house, only more trees lining the pebble road. The car continued to sweep up the road and then in the distance Tatyana saw a mansion sitting on the horizon. Her dreams of twenty seconds ago became more and more real. 'You live here?' she turned to Sarah her eyes as wide as the light would allow.

'Yes. We live here. You'll live here as well now, up until you are able to live on your own.' Sarah smiled.

'Do you have horses?'

'Horses? No. We don't. We used to though. We do have dogs. I hope you like dogs?'

'Yes. I love animals.'

The car pulled to a stop at the side of the house Sarah opened the back door. Tatyana stayed in the back seat staring out the window in disbelief. 'You coming?' Sarah asked as she held her hand out.

'First things first, we'll get you a warm cup of tea and then I'll show you where the bathroom is and where you'll sleep. You'll need some rest.'

Sarah led her through the courtyard into the back door of the mansion and into a beautiful country kitchen. In the middle of the room there was a long wooden table that had chairs for twelve people to comfortably sit. The heat from the range cooker was enough to warm the kitchen. Tatyana sat down at the table as Sarah filled the kettle. 'Are you hungry?' she asked over her shoulder.

'No. I'm ok, thank you. Your kitchen is so nice, how many people live here?'

'Thank you. It is nice, but it's expensive to run. Well, there is my husband Giles, I was hoping he would be here to meet you but his car has gone so he must he away at the minute. We have a daughter called Poppy, she's seven. There's also my mum, she's in a wheelchair and a bit grumpy if you meet her. Don't worry though, her bark is worse than her bite.'

Tatyana smiled. 'You're family sounds lovely.'

'Thank you, we all live here, but there is always people about who help us. Peter, who drove you here, he works with us. He does lots of odd jobs around the house. At any one time we can have other children like yourself that we help, they stay here until they are ready to move out and look after themselves. At the minute we have a couple of other girls, Zusana who is around the same age as you and a slightly younger girl whose name is Anna. You'll meet them later.'

The backdoor creaked open and the driver came in with Tatyana's clothes.

'Ah, speak of the devil...Peter, I'd like to formally introduce you to Tatyana.' Sarah didn't turn her gaze from the tea making duties as she spoke. Peter pulled a beanie hat from his head revealing a closely shaved head and extended his hand to shake Tatyana's. 'Nice to meet you little one, I'm sorry it isn't better circumstances.' His slight lisp was noticeable. Tatyana stood up to shake his hand. She barely came up to his chest and Peter bent slightly to meet her. Tatyana found herself staring at a scar he had on his cheek where the stubble that covered most of his face didn't grow. 'I was a bit of a wild one when I was younger' he winked at and she felt embarrassed for getting caught.

'Uh, thank you for helping me.'

'You're very welcome. You can always come to me for any help you need.'

'Peter, I'm just putting the kettle on, do you want a cup?' Sarah was placing milk and sugar on the table.

'No ma'am, thank you though. I was hoping if you didn't need me I could head on?'

'Yes, absolutely, would you mind checking on the dogs before you go and make sure they've got food? Thank you. We'll see you tomorrow.'

Peter nodded in agreement and left the same way as he came in.

After they finished their tea Sarah showed Tatyana

37

around the house and took her to her room. She had a double bed to herself and a small teddy bear sat propped up against a pillow for her and a clean pair of pyjamas laid out on the duvet.

To the right was a small en-suite with a shower and fresh towels laid over a radiator.

'I suggest you have a shower now before Poppy comes home and takes all the hot water. Tomorrow we'll go out and get you some new clothes. We don't like having a TV in the bedroom here, but there are a few books beside the bed if you want to read. I suspect you'll be tired though.' Sarah was standing in the doorway as Tatyana looked around the room.

'I'm going to nip out for an hour to pick up Poppy, but then I'll be back. Zusana and Anna will be about the house so introduce yourself if you meet them, they know you're coming. Do what you want to, if you want to sleep, go ahead. If you want to come downstairs and watch TV with us, you're welcome to. I know the last few days have been horrible for you, but that's over now. In this room you're safe.' Sarah closed the door softly behind her as she left. She stood at the door for a moment and heard a faint 'thank you.' She smiled and went downstairs.

After Sarah had made dinner and put Poppy to bed she went to the study to go through the bills. Giles still hadn't made it home, which wasn't normal but at least it allowed her to get on with the work that needed done without having another argument. She sat down at the old mahogany desk with her coffee and calculator. The bills were mounting up and their money was being stretched further and further. Sarah had married in to the Marsden family, much to the delight of her mother.

At first, her and Giles were happy and in love, she still loved him now, it was just harder to find at the end of each day. The country manor was left to them by his parents along with a substantial trust fund for its upkeep. Had Giles left it alone they would have been fine. Giles however was a dreamer and like many over the last ten years invested everything they had in the property market draining the trust fund. Times were good until the crash. Now they were left with nothing in the trust fund and twelve properties in total. At the minute they were scraping by hoping for the market to pick up again. If interest rates rise in the next year or two they will most likely lose everything. Poppy would become homeless and they would have to start from scratch. Sarah couldn't let that happen, she mustn't let that happen.

Sarah's mother, Margarite Smyth was now in her 80's and she had moved in with Sarah and Giles seven years ago in what Sarah thought was the pinnacle of her mother's life. Margarite's voice changed when she told delivery men over the phone what her address was, she had definitely moved up in the world. She had raised her daughter the right way, find a man with money. Now confined to a wheelchair she still sat bolt upright in the chair. A ladies' demeanour was so important after-all. Sarah felt the only reason she sat so straight was to make sure she was able to look down at her even from a sitting position.

Sarah had sorted the bills into three piles, 'must pay now,' 'leave a month' and 'ignore for the minute' when the doorbell rang. She checked her watch to confirm that it was indeed as late as she thought it was. Her heart leapt into her throat, Giles. Something's wrong. She peered out the window and saw the police car in the driveway. Her worst fears and dreams were becoming realised all at once. Giles' life insurance would allow her and Poppy to be freed from this burden and weight holding her down, but she loves him. Wholly. No, he can't be dead. Poppy needs him, she needs him.

Sarah shook as she walked downstairs. Her heart and mind were racing in tandem. What will the next five minutes bring, how will she cope? What's he done? Is he dead?

Margarite rolled her wheelchair into the hallway to see what was happening.

"I suppose he's got himself into more trouble"

"Not now mother" Sarah snapped. "Go back to your room, I'll be in with your chocolate shortly"

"Don't talk to you mother like that young lady, don't you forget I brought you into this world…"

"And I brought you into this house, so show me some damn respect and just go back to your room. Christ mother, my marriage is none of your business!"

Sarah stood at the front door waiting for her mother to retreat before she answered. She took two deep breaths to compose herself. As she pulled the heavy wooden door back she saw Giles standing there flanked by two officers. He was grinning like an idiot. Her legs began to give way with relief but she used the door to steady herself.

'Sarah Marsden?' the older of the officers asked.

'Yes?' was all Sarah could reply with. Stuck between wanting to slap Giles and hug him she just stood there.

'Your husband was involved in a car crash this

evening. He has tested positive for driving under the influence and will be required to attend court in the next couple of days.'

'Is he hurt? What happened?'

'He appears to be fine Mrs Marsden, unfortunately we can't say the same for the pedestrian he hit. She has been taken to hospital. An officer will be by in the next day or two with the court summons. The car he was driving is at the police station, it will need picked up as well. Good night.'

Sarah closed the front door and turned to Giles. He was sobering up and the hangover had started early.

'Look, I - ' he didn't get an opportunity to finish as Sarah's palm smacked across his face.

'What? What Giles? Dear God, what on earth have you done now? I'm here trying my best to keep this fucking family afloat and you're away getting pissed somewhere. And as if that's not bad enough you're about to lose your license. So we'll have to give Peter more hours to drive you around you fucking idiot. Oh, I almost forgot, you knocked a woman down. Oh God, you knocked a woman down, I hope to God she is alright. You complete fucking bastard'

Giles had his hands up in defence mode as Sarah swung for him blocking her arm from hitting his face with the first swing but the second arm came from the other side and caught him just above his right eye. 'I swear to fucking God Giles, I could kill you sometimes. I'm drowning here and you're no fucking help at all.'

'I won at the races, almost three thousand. Here.' He pulled a huge wad of notes from his jacket pocket and handed them to her.

'The races! You went to the fucking horses and

gambled our money away…AGAIN. For christ's sake Giles, how many times are you going to do this. You won this time, but last time you lost, the time before that you lost, and the time before that. I distinctly recall having to pay off some particularly scary men last year, or do you not remember? I fucking do. I remember Poppy's face as she opened her Christmas presents that year Giles. I won't see that face again. As for your feeble three grand, you can shove it up your arse, that won't even cover the bills for this month. Oh you're a big help aren't you?'

'Mummy?' Poppy was standing in her pyjamas rubbing her eyes. Sarah stopped instantly.

'Oh sweetie, I'm sorry, did mummy and daddy wake you?' Sarah quickly gave Giles a death stare and then turned her attention to Poppy. She went over to her and picked her up in her arms.

'Why are you and daddy fighting?'

'I'm sorry sweetie, Daddy and I are fighting because Daddy did something really silly, but he was doing it for all of us. It's been a long day for mummy and she's a bit tired. Come on. Give Daddy a kiss and we'll go to bed.'

Poppy leaned over and kissed Giles. 'Night Daddy'

'Night sweetie, sleep tight.'

Sarah took Poppy up to bed without looking behind her leaving Giles standing alone in the hallway.

A mother's manipulation

Margarite sat looking out of the window with her back to the door. The view from her window allowed her to map out her life. She could see in the distance the labourers cottage where she and her sister were born. The manor she now resided in loomed large over her childhood. Her father was a gardener until his hands became too sore to continue to work. In order to keep the family fed she had to leave school and work. She had been lucky and quickly got a job as a seamstress in the factory that just opened. Although it had now changed from a factory to trendy new apartments the footprint was still the same. In the distance she could see a young mum washing her dishes staring out of the kitchen window. Margarite had been that age once too. She had dreamed out the very same window although over seventy years ago it wasn't a window of a loving family home. She wondered if the young mum had the same dreams as she had back then.

The memory brought her back to 1974, Tuesday 5th to be exact. Remember, remember the fifth of November children sang. Margarite could never forget it. It was just after her morning tea break and Margarite was looking over the shoulder of her friend Janette at the droplets of rain on the window when Bernard her line manager asked to see her in his office. She followed him up to the managers' landing and he closed the door and blinds behind him.

'Please, have a seat' Bernard spoke politely as he hung his corduroy jacket on the coat hooks. It smelt of the camel cigarettes that she could see poking out of the side pocket. Bernard was only a year older than she was, but they had been in the same school class together until Margarite had to drop out. Margarite had been naturally bright and curious as a child which meant she excelled in school while she was there. The headmaster had tried his best to keep her in classes but circumstances meant she needed to work.

'Thank you' Margarite was nervous as she spoke, convinced she was in trouble. Her productivity was ok, she seldom missed any targets and there had been no complaints about the quality of her work as far as she knew.

'I'm not sure if you've heard the rumours on the shop floor or not Margarite' Bernard sat on the edge of his mahogany desk as he spoke. She looked blankly at him. 'The company is going through what we in management talk about as a transition period. What this means is that I'm afraid we will have to reduce hours or in some cases let staff go completely.' He remained silent for a long pause to let the information sink in.

'Do you enjoy working here Margarite?'

'Yes'. She didn't but she didn't have any other option either. She needed this job. It was just her and her dad left, and he was sick with no income.

'Good. I like you Margarite, I really do. I'd hate to see you have to leave. Would you like me to put in a good word for you?'

'I can't lose this job.'

Bernard stood and came closer to her. He stroked her left cheek with the back of his hand as he talked. Margarite could still feel his wedding ring slide across her face to this very day.

'I can't just put in a good word for anyone, you'd need to make it worth my while' his hand dropped from her face and he started to grope her breast. Margarite froze. Her mind was racing, should she slap him? Should she scream? She did neither. Her indecision was seen as complicitness and Bernard moved in front of her to kiss her. His moustache was still wet from his earlier coffee and his breath was a combination of that and camel cigarettes. Margarite was in her late thirties in 1974 but she had never had a boyfriend and wasn't married. Her time was spent caring for her father. The opposite sex were still a mystery to her. She had missed out on a lot of social learning when she left school.

Margarite kept her mouth closed as he continued to kiss her, resisting in the most passive way she could. She didn't have control of the situation but she could have control of aspects of it. Bernard pulled her on to the floor of his office and put his hand up her skirt. Her body stiffened as his fingers traced higher up the inside of her thigh. She regretted not wearing any tights. The factory floor was warm despite the temperature outside. Her passive resistance had now completely subsided as she lay on the floor, Bernard's breath heavy in her ear as he thrusted. A tear came to her eye as she stared at the nicotine patched ceiling, waiting for him to finish.

Sarah's knock at her door brought her back to the present day.

'Come in love, I was just thinking about your father' Margarite continued to stare out the window as she spoke. 'If only he could see you now, living here.'

'I'm sure he saw plenty in his time in the army.' Sarah was now standing beside her mum holding a cup of hot chocolate which was her night time ritual.

'He died from a pipe bomb in Derry, I told you that, didn't I?' She had kept the lie for the whole of Sarah's life. Too ashamed to tell her. Bernard still lived close by. His wife had passed from cancer many years ago and he lived alone now. They had never had children and Margarite wasn't going to let him have any part of her daughters life.

'Yes mum, he was going to be made a captain but died trying to save his team. Here, have some chocolate.' Sarah had heard the story often but superficially. She had stopped asking questions in her early teens as her mother would often clam up and not talk, or start shouting when there was a question she couldn't answer. Sarah knew there was more to the story that she didn't know.

'I see a lot of your father in Giles my dear.'

Sarah let out a long sigh. 'Speaking of, my marriage is my marriage mum. You cannot keep butting in. We invited you to live with us. Giles invited you to live with us. I know you don't really like him but he is a good man, he's just a bit lost at the minute. I love him and I'll stand by him.'

'Please sit a minute'

'I can't mum, I need to go and see Poppy - '

'Just a minute, it won't take long.'

Sarah reluctantly sat on the floor. Her mother was obstinate at the best of times but as she aged the fights and fall outs were just not worth it. Sarah had a very good idea of where this conversation was going, she was hearing it more and more recently. Margarite knew she was on her last lap and had lots to repair from years of constant fighting with each other, she just didn't know how to.

Their relationship was troublesome to say the least, Sarah had always felt as though there was nothing she could have done to please her mum. She was a straight A student. Not good enough. She was captain of the local hockey team. Not good enough. She was a leader in the church. Not good enough. Every time Sarah came home there was 'the look'. Something she could not understand until she was older, but the only way she could describe it was as though her own mother was ashamed of her. She knew it was silly, her mother loved her, but still, she couldn't shake the feeling. It drove Sarah more than she cared to admit. She wanted to be flippant and ambivalent to it, but she couldn't. It was probably why she fought so hard to keep the manor house. If they sold it and bought a simple three bed semi they would be free. But freedom wouldn't make Margarite less ashamed. Sarah knew the pride Margarite had when she spoke of the house.

'I know you and I haven't had the best of times Sarah' Margarite spoke to the window without looking at her daughter. 'I know I could have been a better mum. It's just…' she trailed off.

They both sat in silence. Sarah waited. It was the same old story. Her mother making things about herself. Taking her time away from her own daughter.

'We can talk about this in the morning mum. Good night.' Sarah stood up and kissed her mum on the forehead before leaving. As she reached the door her mum called out.

'Sarah?'

'Yes mum' she sighed still holding on to the handle.

Margarite hesitated. Looking for the right words. They didn't come. 'I'm glad you never smoked'.

'OK' Sarah left muttering to herself as Margarite slumped in her wheelchair with a tear coming down her cheek.

A lesser sentence

The unused cot lay broken in the corner of the nursery Remi had almost finished. All it needed was a final coat of yellow paint and then the oak skirting boards applied. His plan had been to finish the work this weekend giving them a couple of weeks rest before their daughter arrived. There was no need to now. He sat on the floor staring ahead at nothing in particular with the paint tin between his legs. Laura hated when he called it yellow paint, she said it made it sound like it came from a health and safety brochure. Lemon Spirit was its correct colour. Periodically he drank from the beer bottle that had long since turned lukewarm. He finished the last swig of the beer and threw it against the wall in anger and frustration. The bottle smashed instantly and the wall was splashed with beer as it trickled down the paint, matching the tears on his face.

The doorbell rang but Remi didn't move. Whoever it was would come back when he was in the mood. Whenever that would be. It rang again. He ignored it again. Moments later he heard the lock turning and the door opening. 'Remi?' it was Louise's voice. 'We're coming in' He didn't answer they would find him soon enough. Remi listened as the team walked through the house underneath him finding nothing. Next her heard footsteps on the stairs, only one set. Then came a gentle tap on the door, 'Remi, honey, you in here?' Louise poked her head around the door and surveyed the scene. Her heart sank even further than it already was.

She didn't have the words that were needed so she chose not to say anything, went over, got on her knees and hugged her friend. After a few moments of silence she let go and sat beside Remi, looking ahead at the damage in front of her as she spoke. 'We heard, I'm so, so sorry. We came straight over. The whole force is with you on this, we'll get the fucker.'

Remi didn't reply. He just sat there staring at the wall. Louise didn't try and interrupt the silence.

'Doesn't matter.' He spoke finally. 'Doesn't matter at all Lou. Won't bring her back, it won't make me a dad. It won't rebuild our dreams.' Remi stood up and offered his hand to his boss. 'Thanks for coming over.'

'The guys are downstairs, whatever you need.'

Remi nodded and Louise followed him down to the kitchen. Ben and Sam were sitting at the table having a quiet conversation that stopped as soon as Remi came in. Sam stood up, went over to Remi and hugged him. No words were spoken. Ben sat in his chair half turned to face Remi not knowing what to do, this was the first time he had ever experienced death in any way. He was only learning how to react. Remi sat beside the younger man and rubbed his head as he pulled out a chair to acknowledge his being there.

'I'm sorry I've no food, we could order a Chinese?' Remi spoke to them all.

'Tom made a lasagne, I'll put it in the oven.' Louise

responded over her shoulder as she was already removing the tinfoil.

'Jesus Lou, if you weren't married to him, I'd marry that man. He really is a saint.' There was a hollowness to Remi's voice as he spoke.

'He sends his love, the kids do too.' Louise's words fell over the table as they sat in silence, looking for some comfort that would never come.

'I dunno if I'd marry him, I like lasagne, but it's not my favourite.' Everyone turned and looked at Ben who instantly regretted speaking. He felt the need to clarify. 'I mean I'd date him, but he'd need a few other recipes to get me to ask the question.' Sam shot him a look of shut up, but the words were already out. There was a split second of silence and then Remi burst into laughter, the kind of laughter that comes from a combination of tiredness and relief of finding a sliver of normality. They all joined in.

'Well I'm glad you aren't going to steal my husband over a lasagne Ben'

'Can he make a curry?'

'You'll never know if it means that I'll find you sending him text messages late at night.' Louise sat down at the table and handed them a beer each. 'To our friend and his family, some stars are too bright for this world.' All four of them tapped their bottles together and took a swig. It was a ritual they enjoyed many times together but this was the first time no-one smiled as they did so.

The text message broke the silence as they ate Tom's lasagne which was so delicious Ben was wavering on his stance on marriage. Louise checked her phone and quickly excused herself from the table. When she came back her face was pale.

'What's wrong?'   Remi asked before she could compose herself and think of a way to break the news.

'What's up boss?' Ben asked putting his fork down.

'That was the chief, he's just off the phone with the prosecutor. Remi there's no way to break this easily.' Louise stood temporarily frozen as she looked Remi in the eye. 'They're reducing the charge. He's only being charged with 'death by careless driving under the influence'

'BULLSHIT!' Sam was outraged.

'Won't bring her back Sam.' Remi was numb as he picked up his plate and went to the kitchen to clean up. 'I've been sitting all day plotting revenge, hoping I get to kill him myself or that he'll be locked away for good. But you know what, my duty is to bury my wife and daughter. Nothing more. The courts will decide what his punishment is. How many times have we seen and arrested people who went after revenge. We do this job because we believe in justice. He'll get justice, it's up to me to accept it. It's not up to me to define it.'

'You don't really believe that' although Sam's voice was back to normal levels, there was still frustration behind his words.

'I have to Sam, I have to'. Remi was absent as he spoke. In his mind he was holding Laura on the sofa and rubbing her bump.

The Courthouse

Rain slid down the inside of Remi's collar as he walked up the steps to the courthouse. It was mid-morning and he'd been up for at least eight hours already. The bags under his eyes were getting bigger daily. He had found it hard to sleep over the last couple of weeks when Laura was restless beside him. It was nigh on impossible now she wasn't there.

The days and weeks following death were brutal. Remi had seen it many times through work. People go through the motions; they meet others who want to offer condolences, they answer questions. The same questions over and over again. They perform duties, put on a show. It keeps them going in the initial stages.

This was different. This was his first time experiencing it for himself. Living in the grief vacuum. The vacuum shields you. It enables you to function. Only once all your tasks are complete; Paperwork. Funeral. Visitors. Burials. Court trials. Your commitment to your loved ones, unspoken promises that were made between you. Only once they have been done and you sit down in your empty house alone. Only then does the vacuum open a small hole and let grief come to sit with you. Silence its messenger.

If you're smart you'll allow it to come. You'll welcome it and sit with it, embrace it. Enjoy the company, almost. If you're not smart you'll avoid it. You'll do everything you can to ignore its existence. You'll keep busy. You'll take on more work. You'll lie to yourself. Grief will wait, but it won't be ignored. It knows the difference, even when you don't.

Remi wanted to be anywhere other than the courthouse, but he had a duty to his family. His grief waited. An invisible black fog stalking the corridors anxious to talk to him. He'd been to court a few times before as a witness. Normally he didn't mind, it was a fairly easy day, you just had to wait to be called, go in and talk through what you saw. It was rarely as dramatic as the TV shows Laura had loved watching. She often asked him about what court was like. Without fail his recollections always disappointed her.

Today was different. He hadn't waited near the courthouse. He struggled to pass the time in a coffee shop round the corner. Louise was at the courts. She'd resisted arguing he needed to be there. She had wanted Sam or Ben to be with Remi but he wouldn't let them. It would be hard enough waiting without having to make small talk. Remi had a point and they'd agreed she would phone him when the case was due to be called. This was the simplest way. There wouldn't be enough police to hold Remi back if he was forced to sit in the same room as Giles Marsden longer than necessary.

Remi hadn't reached the top of the steps when Louise came to meet him. He handed her the large latte he'd bought en-route.

'Thanks.' She took a sip. 'Better than the vending

machine'

'How long?'

'Only a couple of minutes now most likely.' She took another sip before continuing 'Listen, there's some bad news...'

'What?'

She looked in his broken eyes and searched for the words that wouldn't come. She took his elbow in her hand and tried to lead him to a quieter corner even though it was just the two of them. He shrugged her hand away.

'Damn it Lou, what is it?'

'Something - '

'Just spit it out, I don't need sugarcoating. There can't be anymore bad news.'

'The paperwork...' Louise stopped and closed her eyes. She couldn't look at her friend. 'The paperwork was incomplete. They've reduced the sentence to 'causing death by careless or inconsiderate driving.'

'Paperwork? That doesn't make sense. Just re-submit. It happens all the time.'

'It still carries a custodial sentence Remi. They have to lock him up.'

'What the hell happened?'

'I dunno, I only got the news this morning. I didn't want to tell you over the phone.'

'Lou? Remi? It's us.' Sam called over from a respectable distance.

'Let's just see how this goes, huh? Come on, take my arm.' She slipped her arm into his and looked up at his face, but it was distant. They started to walk together into the courtroom when Remi stopped in his tracks.

Giles Marsden was wearing a neck brace with

multiple lawyers circling him. He looked different from how Remi remembered him in broad daylight. Weaker somehow. He was a tall man, almost as tall as Remi but unlike Remi he couldn't carry it off. His frame was slight which meant his clothes hung off him waiting for him to fill them. His hair was curly and thinning at the top and when he turned to the side he had a hooked nose that Louise confirmed was easily a half size too big for his face.

The smirk he'd worn in the back of the police car was replaced with a sombre look that Remi could only see as practised.

Giles was holding hands with a woman and young girl holding a teddy bear. The girl was terrified. So many adults stood around her dad. All talking in words she didn't understand. Her look wasn't practised.

'His family?' Remi nodded at the woman and young girl.

'Apparently so' Louise replied staring directly at them. 'What kind of a prick brings his daughter to something like this?'

'A calculating one. Who's the judge?'

'Reinholdt'

Giles felt Remi's presence in the foyer. He turned the long way round to avoid eye contact in order to speak to Sarah. 'It'll be alright'. He reassured his wife. 'It was an accident.' Sarah looked up at her husband. He really was naive. 'Yes, sweetheart.' She reached up and straightened the collar on his jacket. 'I really wish you hadn't worn your dad's jacket. It looks ridiculous on you.'

'Not now Sarah.' She'd made her point so didn't push the issue. Instead she reached on her tiptoes and gave him a peck on the cheek. Giles leaned into the kiss but didn't respond. He turned to his daughter and leaned down so he could talk to her. 'Poppet, everything is going to be ok'. Poppy squeezed her dad tightly unable to articulate her fear. Her tears came quickly as she held on to her dad for reassurance he couldn't give.

Remi watched the scene unfolding in front of him. It was a stark reminder of a stolen future. He waited for the Marsdens to go into the courtroom first. After a moment he took a deep breath to calm himself as he walked through the door and took a seat beside Sam, his eyes focused on the Marsden family but bore into Giles's skull. Louise wordlessly shuffled him up so she could sit down effectively penning him in. No one said a word.

'All rise'

Arrogance

The courtroom had now emptied and Remi sat alone with his thoughts. His mind leapt second by second. From rage at what he'd just seen to shame at feeling he'd let Laura down. Let his daughter down. He swallowed his emotions as it suddenly hit him that they hadn't settled on a name. He had fallen in love and he didn't even know her name. He hadn't been able to get them justice. Get them something, anything. Their memory deserved more than this. Ultimately though he settled on emptiness. He sat staring ahead, vacant, hoping Laura would somehow walk through the door and take him home. Hold him. He hoped he would go home tonight and they would have dinner, or they would argue over what to watch on TV. Something, anything to prove that this was all a dream. He swallowed again. He was exhausted. A wave of tiredness hit his bones. Tears welled up in his eyes as his grief sidled up beside him, ready for its moment.

He barely heard the door open as Louise came in. She said nothing as she sat down but saw the broken piece of the seat directly in front of Remi about the size of a fist. His grief vanished as he wiped his eyes. Its opportunity missed.

'You know, my whole life I've believed that no matter what happens there is justice'. Remi stared ahead as he spoke. 'We have laws and rules that govern society, we, the police uphold the law and the courts administer justice. We know it's not perfect, we know it could be better but we accept that when we sign up. But this? This can't be justice?' he turned, his face wet with tears, red eyes pleading with Louise.

'We're all too close to this. There is no sentence that would have been enough'.

'But suspended, Lou? Suspended sentence. He gets to kiss his daughter goodnight tonight. What do I get?'

He was right. Louise's heart ached for her friend. She hadn't felt this helpless since her and Tom had sat in A&E with their youngest as he'd got a lumbar puncture to test for meningitis. 'We'll get him, sooner or later, guys like this…they get what's coming to them. We'll get him'. Her words were as empty as the room they sat in and they both knew it.

Outside Ben was absentmindedly fingering the packet of cigarettes in his pocket debating whether he could get a smoke in before Louise and Remi came out. He had watched Giles and Sarah argue wordlessly in the foyer. Giles and gone to hug her but she kept her arms folded, disgust dripping from her very core. Moments later she had taken the young girl and stormed off and Giles had retreated to the bathroom. A sharp nudge to his ribs made his nicotine decision for him. He'd have to wait. 'What?'

'Look who that is'. Sam exaggerated a nod forward indicating where to look. Ben spotted instantly. 'Our little van driver'. The young man who they had caught smuggling fuel was sitting on a bench in the foyer waiting with his lawyer. Dressed in a rented suit he slouched while playing on his phone ignorant of the world around him. His lawyer stood up and went to talk to Giles Marsden's lawyers. They welcomed each other warmly and stood chatting for a while.

'Jesus. Their clients may run in different circles but the lawyers definitely don't. They look like old school pals'. Ben checked his watch as he passed judgment. The only response from Sam was a grunt. The toilet door opened and Giles Marsden walked out, his neck brace now removed and sombre mood replaced with casual ambivalence which suited his face more readily.

'You absolute...'

'Leave it'. Sam grabbed Ben's arm to keep him in place.

Giles reached his lawyers and shook the hand of the van drivers representation. As he spoke with them the young van driver looked up from his phone and hurriedly put it in his pocket. He stopped slouching and sat up straight fully alert to those around him now.

'Thanks for coming guys'. Remi's voice came from behind them. Ben and Sam both spun round to face him a little too quickly. 'What's up?' Remi was looking behind them as best he could but they both shifted slightly to block his view.

'Nothing. Come on. Let's get out of here bud'. Ben went to lead him away but was shrugged away. Remi had seen what they were trying to hide.

'Shit'. Louise had spotted as well. 'Remi, don't. He's not worth...' Sam and Ben both jumped in front of Remi and started to hold him back but it was too late. The emptiness that had settled inside before had been extinguished by rage. The sight of Giles' neck open without the support of the brace he so desperately needed while he sat inside the courtroom was too much and Remi had had enough. It was enough that this man had killed his family intentionally or not. It was enough that this man had walked out of court without so much as a slap on the wrist but for him to stand in the foyer and flaunt his lies in his face. That was too much. Remi was walking with pace and purpose. Sam and Ben were doing their best to hold him but they couldn't. They were slowing him down, marginally at best. In a few seconds they had reached the group of lawyers who were between Giles and Remi. The lawyers stood frozen for a split second. Giles turned and saw Remi. It wasn't good but he was protected. Remi couldn't get past Ben and Sam as well as the lawyers. So Giles thought. In an instant Remi's massive hand reached over Ben and Sam, dissected the lawyers and grabbed Giles by the throat knocking two of the lawyers out of the way as it did so. This gave Remi the space he needed. He continued forward, his grip not once leaving the neck of Giles whose casual ambivalence had been replaced with blind terror. Two more steps and Giles was pinned against a wall. The huddle of lawyers had now split like bowling pins. Ben and Sam were still between him and Remi although they didn't have much say in what they were doing. Each of the lawyers stepped back further watching from what they perceived was a safe distance.

'Sore neck? Feels fine to me' Remi squeezed even tighter and Giles choked and gasped for some air, his toes barely tickling the ground. The voices in the background telling Remi to 'leave it' 'he's not worth it' 'you'll go down for this' all subsided in the distance as he focussed solely on the man who killed his wife and unborn daughter.

Around him became still. Remi could snap his neck with one hand. His grip tightened even more. Then he heard a voice, calling him. It was Laura's. Calling in his heart. 'This isn't you darling. This isn't the man I married'. He loosened his grip on Giles' neck, enough for him to breathe but still held him.

The punch came from nowhere, it barely phased Remi but it was enough for him to let go of Giles' neck as he turned to see where it had come from. Giles slumped to the floor and gathered himself as quickly as he could to get out of reach. Ben and Sam took their opportunity and pulled Remi away from the chaos he'd created.

'Christ Remi. I know you're hurting, but GBH in front of lawyers?' Louise shouted in a whisper as though doing so kept what everyone had just witnessed a secret.

Giles had recovered sufficiently to regather himself with his lawyers. He nervously looked over at Remi who hadn't taken his eyes off him despite moving backwards at glacial pace. It was clear that Remi wasn't leaving the foyer first.

Giles stood for a moment smoothing his tweed jacket and fixing his tie in an effort to appear unperturbed while the predator he had angered stalked his every move. Unable to fix his tie any more without choking himself more than Remi had two minutes previously Giles went over to the young van driver who had intervened on his behalf and shook his hand.

'Thank you young man. I appreciate your help from such a *thug*'

'Anytime Mr Marsden'.   Giles froze almost imperceptibly at the mention of his name and had Remi not been paying attention so intently he wouldn't have picked up on it. But he was.

'Quite. Well I must be off. Good luck to you'.

Remi's stare followed Giles leaving the foyer and into the main street with his two lawyers. Once he was sure he'd gone the stare turned its focus on the young van driver who remained rooted to the spot. Alone with just his lawyer the van driver averted his eyes from Remi and sat back down. He pulled the mobile phone out of his pocket and began playing again.

Some strings

Tatyana woke with a start. Panic gripped her. *Where am I?* Her hands reached out around her. Softness. Warmth. She turned under the duvet, light that filtered under the gap in the curtains attacked her eyes. She pulled the duvet over her head as a shield. As she lay under the duvet the panic subsided and she began to remember, she was free. Sarah had come for her. She had climbed into bed last night and slept. A deep sleep. For the first time in what had felt like months she had slept. Not a fitful sleep, a restorative sleep. She pulled the duvet down from over her head and kicked her legs with excitement releasing a smile that had been long forgotten. She stopped kicking and turned over and over wrapping herself in the duvet. As the tightness of the duvet enveloped her, memories of her grandmother wrapping her in a towel after a bath every Sunday flooded her brain. She lay her head back on the pillow allowing the memory to stay with her. It was one of the few memories she had that were happy.

Tatyana had never known her mother, she had died in childbirth with Tatyana. Her father never got over her death, or maybe he never forgave Tatyana. She wasn't sure which but it meant her and her two older brothers had been raised by their maternal grandmother until she passed away when Tatyana was ten. Sunday was Tatyana's favourite day in the whole week. Her brothers would go out with their dad so Tatyana was able to spend time with her grandmother all alone. Most days she would help with dinner for when the boys came back. She would sit with her grandmother at the table and shell peas or peel potatoes. It didn't matter. What she loved most was to hear the stories of when her mother was a little girl. She often wondered what she was like. Would she have loved me? She always asked her grandmother. 'Without a doubt' came the reply every time, without fail.

Footsteps outside the bedroom banished her fond memories. Fear returned and gripped her body as her mind was brought back to her brothers visiting her bedroom at night. After her grandmother passed away her dad drank more and more and the children were left to fend for themselves. Playing at grown ups. Badly. At first Tatyana didn't understand what was happening when her eldest brother came into her bedroom. She had just turned twelve and enjoyed the attention she desperately needed. She quickly stopped enjoying it as he began to touch her. The next day she told her dad what happened before her brothers came home from school. Drunkenly he had beaten them both that night but by the time morning came he'd forgotten. Her brothers hadn't and Tatyana had paid dearly for their bruises.

She sat frozen on the bed remaining wrapped in the duvet. Naively she hoped it would provide some protection for what was coming. The footsteps stopped outside the door. She scanned the room quickly to see if there was anything she could use to defend herself. The was a gentle knock on the door. Tatyana remained silent, her fear holding back any words. 'Tatyana?' the voice was soft. Sarah's head appeared from the half open door and Tatyana released the breath she hadn't realised she was holding.

'Sorry, I didn't mean to wake you'.

'It's OK, I was awake'. Tatyana was trying to unravel herself from the feather down cocoon she had created as Sarah came into the room carrying a tray with breakfast on it.

'I hope you're hungry. I brought breakfast to you this time but tomorrow you'll join us downstairs. I wasn't sure what you wanted but here's tea and toast'. She left the tray on the bed, went to the window and pulled back the curtains. Light flooded the room. 'There's a clean towel in the drawer, have a shower, get changed and when you're ready bring your tray downstairs. I'll be waiting and we'll go out and get you some clothes that actually fit, ok?'

Tatyana muffled a thank you through the toast that filled her mouth.

'You're welcome sweetheart.'

When Tatyana finished her shower there was a pile of clothes on the bed for her. A pair of grey tracksuit bottoms, a t-shirt and a pastel pink hoody. All of which were too big for her but that didn't matter. After two showers and hot meals in 24 hours Tatyana felt like a movie star. She put the clothes on and started to make her way to the kitchen. The corridors seemed to be a labyrinth as she carried her tray hoping to see a door she remembered. The air in the corridors felt dense as though all the molecules had huddled together over the years waiting for someone to open a window and free them. But the windows remained shut and the air had grown stale and heavy. Tatyana tried not to cough and spill the tray as she walked. Eventually she saw a large door that looked familiar and went through. Inside Giles Marsden was standing in his boxer shorts getting changed.

'Sorry, I'm so sorry'. Immediately Tatyana apologised and turned to leave.

Giles turned and smiled standing in just his underwear. 'It's OK. Please come in. I'm Giles, you must be Tatyana. Sarah has told me about you.'

Tatyana held her gaze to the floor as she spoke. 'Hello. Yes, I'm Tatyana. I'm sorry I was looking for the kitchen.' Giles moved closer and held her chin gently as he lifted her head slightly.

'It's very nice to meet you Tatyana. I do hope you enjoy your stay with us.' He continued to hold her chin as he spoke. He paused in silence as if lost in thought as he eyed Tatyana's face. After a moment he continued. 'The kitchen is to the left, down the stairs and it's the second door on the right.' He removed his hand from her chin letting his thumb caress her cheek as he did so. Tatyana stood waiting to be dismissed. 'Go on now, I'll see you down there. I can't be walking about the house in my underwear now can I?'

Tatyana didn't have an answer so she just turned and left, pulling the door shut behind her. After a couple of wrong turns she finally heard Sarah boiling the kettle and knocked on the door before she entered.

'Come in sweetheart' Sarah was sitting at the table going through the post. 'Just leave the tray on the counter. Was there enough hot water?' she asked while frowning at a brown envelope.

'Yes, thank you'. Tatyana placed the tray on the counter and stood beside it, not knowing what to do next.

'Good. Now I didn't know what shoe size you were so I want you to go with Zusana and Anna, they'll help you get something that fits until I can take you out this afternoon. Girls?' her voice raised at the end to call in the girls whom Tatyana hadn't met yet.

'Yes mama?' both girls appeared at the door together as though they had been waiting in the hall to be called. Tatyana thought they were both beautiful. Anna was taller and as a result looked older, she was maybe seventeen. She had straight jet black hair that came down just past her shoulders. Zusana didn't have the confidence that Anna possessed and it was obvious that Anna was the leader of the two of them as she came over to introduce them both with Zusana hanging behind her left shoulder.

'Girls, Tatyana will be staying with us for a while and I want you to look after her and show her the ropes. I'll be taking her shopping later, can either of you lend her a pair of shoes until then?'

'Yes mama. I'm sure we can find something that will fit.' Anna answered for them both. There was a short silence then Sarah nodded to Anna.

'Come on, we'll see what we can find for you.' Anna took Tatyana by the hand and led her out of the kitchen, closely followed by Zusana.

Both Zusana and Tatyana sat on Anna's bed as Anna went through her wardrobe. 'What size of feet do you have?' Anna's head was deep in the wardrobe as she asked.

'Eh, 38 or 39'

'We should have something then. Where are you from? Zusana and I are from Slovakia'.

'Belarus. Did Sarah help you as well?'

'Ah. Try these'. A pair of grey and orange nikes landed on Tatyana's lap. 'Yes, Sarah helped us. We came here to have a better life than the one we left. We do have a better life, but we are working for an even better one.'

'What do you do?' Tatyana asked as she put the trainer on her left foot.

'Mama is an important lady. She has many friends. We are there to help her friends, and Mama'.

Tatyana stopped tying her shoe laces and looked up at Anna. Her face was filled with questions. Anna shrugged her shoulders and went back to her wardrobe. Tatyana looked to Zusana for answers but none came. The girl dropped her eyes to the floor and hugged her knees to her chest. Tatyana recognised something in Zusana she hoped she'd left behind in Belarus. Now she wasn't so sure.

What's going on?

Inspector Bradley stroked his greying temples as he sat at his desk. He'd been doing so for at least three minutes now. Louise stood on the other side of the desk, she knew better than to interrupt. She had brought her boss up to speed with the courtcase although he already knew. For the moment this is how the man thought. History had been on his side more often than not so it was best to leave him to it.

'I want you to take Remi with you to the fundraiser on Saturday. In fact bring the rest of the team as well, just in case you need them'. Bradley had dropped his fingers from his temples to his mouth and was sitting back in his chair now, almost daring Louise to challenge him.

'I don't think Remi is in the right frame of mind to go to a fundraiser sir. To be honest none of us are.' Louise stood her ground.

'Maybe not. But he has Marsden in his sights now. Nothing will get past him. You think you can keep him under control?' Bradley leaned forward emphasising the question to Louise.

Before she could answer she heard Remi's voice booming across the station. 'Who fucked up?' 'Who fucked up?'

'Shit. We're about to find out!' Louise turned and opened the door to Bradley's office. 'Remi. In here now. That's an order!' Her eyes locked on Remi's. She was not messing around. Within a minute she had closed the door and Remi was standing in silence beside her facing Bradley in his chair.

'Wallace, I'm sorry for your loss. Truly, I am. What you're going through now, no-one should ever have to experience.' Bradley's words had a genuineness in them as he spoke.

'Thank you sir.' Remi's voice was softer now.

'That said. I have higher expectations of any officer in my command. Including you.' Bradley had stood up from his chair walking to the same side of his desk as Remi as he spoke . 'This station will not be treated like a bar where you've come to settle a score, do you understand?'

Remi nodded, suitably scolded. Bradley lowered his tone and continued. 'You are currently on compassionate leave. You'd be wise to take it.'

'I prefer to work sir.' Remi responded to the inferred question.' I can't face an empty house at the minute.' He hadn't meant to say the second part out loud, but he had now. His reply took Louise by surprise, she had never known Remi to show any form of vulnerability. She had to fight back her own tears as she looked at her friend. She considered his profile as he stared forward to a spot high on the back wall avoiding eye contact with either of them. He'd aged in the last couple of days. His eyes were heavy with lack of sleep and his crows feet were more pronounced. But it was more than that, Remi was standing in front of her and he looked exactly how she imagined he felt. Numb.

'I appreciate your honesty Wallace. Both of you, please take a seat. Let's see if we can get to the bottom of this.' Bradley half turned and hit the button on his intercom. 'Sandra? Can you bring me in the rota for the last two weeks please. And three coffees.'

Bradley's PA, Sandra teetered on high heels that were borderline inappropriate for a workplace as she set the tray of coffee down on the table. She gave Remi an empathetic smile as she handed Bradley the staff rota.

Bradley flicked through rota as Louise poured the coffee. A succession of non committal noises emanated from behind the rota. Both Louise and Remi looked at each other blankly.

'I think I've seen the issue.' Bradley spoke as he passed the rota to Louise.

'What?' Remi leaned over to see the rota.

'Tony Knowles was on duty that night'. Bradley answered.

'Knowles? I thought he was off on sick at the minute?' Remi asked Bradley.

'Not sick, carers leave. He's working shorter hours. In one day off four until further notice.'

'I don't understand' Louise had now joined the conversation having set the rota down. 'Just because he's on shorter hours doesn't mean that he'd file the incorrect paperwork. Knowles is a good officer, he wouldn't make a mistake like that'

'I've never worked with him, but I've only heard good things, doesn't seem right'. Remi agreed and was now flicking through the rota.

'You're both right, Knowles is a good officer. But between these four walls he's facing some difficulties at home which may be affecting his work.' Bradley took a sip of his coffee as he contemplated divulging Knowles' personal information. By the time he set his mug back on the table he'd made up his mind. 'This goes no further than these four walls, understood?'

Both Remi and Louise nodded in silent agreement.

'Knowles has a fourteen year old daughter who has a brain tumour. Unfortunately she's not responding well to treatment at the minute.'

'Shit. That's tough'. Louise empathised. Remi grunted. Unable to see past his own troubles at the minute.

'Leave this with me Wallace. I'll pull the paperwork and have a discussion with Knowles when he's next on duty. You'll be the first person I call after. OK?'

'Thanks Sir.' Remi stood to leave.

'Sit. I haven't finished with you both yet.' Bradley waited for Remi to sit before he spoke again. 'Before you came into the station today I was speaking with your team leader about the possibility of you attending a fundraiser on Friday night Wallace. On duty, with your team. Dress uniform. What are your thoughts?

'Not a chance'. Remi spoke first then became more diplomatic as he registered Bradley's look. 'What I mean is, I don't think I'm the best person to be socialising currently, sir.'

'The fundraiser is for "Better Routes" the anti trafficking charity run by Sarah Marsden, wife of Giles Marsden and will be held at Marsden castle. If, and I repeat if, you can behave yourself I think you may be the best person to send. Ms Massey here thinks I'm making a mistake, what do you think?'

'I'm in.' Remi was determined. Louise shook her

head. 'Remi, this isn't the right time. You'll be looking for a fight, I just think —'

'What Lou? you just think what? I think I need a night out. You don't?'

'That's not what I said and you know it.'

'Good.' Remi sat up straighter, feeling justified.

'Mr Wallace.' Bradley interjected. 'This is strictly no drinking and you aren't allowed to go within 50 yards of Giles Marsden. You will be there to observe. And observe only. Understood?'

'Yessir'

'That's all.'

Remi got up to leave. As he reached the door Bradley called to him, 'If you fuck this up Remi I'll not be lenient on you. I'm going against the advice of your team lead. I expect I won't regret doing it.' Remi said nothing as he left the room leaving Bradley and Louise to their coffee.

'We'll keep an eye on him sir'

'I hope you do'

The bailiffs

Poppy Marsden sat at the dinner table picking at the food on her plate. She knew her mum and dad were fighting. They always were. The silence of unspoken anger in the room bore down upon her and added a weight to her heart that she couldn't remember living without.

'May I be excused?' She asked while not looking up.

'Yes sweetie,' 'No pet, please finish your dinner'. Giles and Sarah couldn't even agree on this. Poppy just sighed and slumped back in her chair. All three returned to their own worlds briefly. Sarah broke first.

'Poppy, sweetheart. Sometimes when mummies and daddies live together they don't always get along but that doesn't mean they don't love each other. Daddy and I are trying our best to make sure you have a good and loving home. This home. I know you don't understand at the minute but one day you will.'

Poppy remained slumped, her only focus was moving the peas on her plate from one side to the other. Sarah nodded to Giles to say something. He didn't get the message. 'Isn't that right, Daddy?' Her eyes pleading with her husband, deliberating spelling it out for Giles as he shoved a fork into his mouth. The hint was like a fly at a window with Giles, smacking his face but not making progress. It shouldn't be this hard, she thought.

Poppy stayed slumped but lifted her eyes from her peas to her Dad. Sarah looked intently at Giles. Eyes boring into him to help her. Help his daughter, help his family. Finally, the window opened.

'You see poppet, sometimes…'. There was a knock at the front door as Giles started to speak. 'I'll get it. The relief clearly visible on Giles' face.' Poppy dropped her eyes back to her plate as Giles pushed his chair back to get up.

'You expecting someone?' Sarah asked

'No.' Giles was almost out of the kitchen as he spoke.

The knock came again.

'Coming!' Giles' voice could be heard in the hallway followed by the clunk of the front door snib being unlocked.

The voices were muffled and Sarah couldn't hear what they were saying. 'Stay here sweetheart, mummy is going to see who that is.'

Poppy slumped even further in her chair and threw her fork on the plate. Sarah ignored this and chased Giles into the hall.

'Giles? What's the matter?'

'Nothing. Just go back to dinner darling'. He had blocked the front door so Sarah couldn't see the visitors, but he only ever called her darling whenever he wanted to put on a front. Something was wrong. Sarah pushed in beside him to see.

'Mrs Marsden?' The man with the clipboard was heavy set. Giles was tall but this man dwarfed him and going by the bulges in his shirt he was used to spending more time in the gym than Giles, not that that would be difficult. The two others that flanked him weren't as big physically but they gave the impression that they weren't used to not getting what they wanted.

'Yes. What's the matter?'

'Mrs Marsden, my name is Simon Stones and these two gentlemen are my associates. There is an outstanding debt of thirteen hundred pounds on an Apple MacBook computer that was bought three months ago. We've sent three letters with no response. We're here to collect the computer and any other items that will recover the cost.'

Sarah fired a look at Giles. 'Cash. You said you paid cash for that. You won the cash at the horses. That's Poppy's computer.' The realisation sunk in as she spoke. Her hands went to stop the words leaving her mouth as though it would stop what was happening. 'Oh God, that's Poppy's computer.'

'Mummy? Is everything ok? Poppy had come into the hallway.

Sarah looked directly at Giles as she spoke. 'No. No sweetie, everything is not ok.'

"What's wrong?' Poppy didn't move from the kitchen door. Sarah didn't take her eyes off Giles. He'd have to break the news to her.

'Poppet, you'll have to get your computer for Daddy'. Giles had started to walk towards Poppy's bedroom.

'Why? That's my computer. What have I done?' Poppy was screaming at Giles as she followed him down the corridor.

Sarah stood at the front door. She was broken. She closed her eyes and the tears that had welled up broke free sliding silently down her cheek. She wiped them away and turned to Simon. 'You'll get what you need. Can you give us twenty minutes, half an hour?'

'Of course ma'am. We'll wait in the car. Ideally you'll come to us before then, if not we'll have to come in. We also need to take a TV as well to cover the cost of the insurance that was taken out as well. I'm sorry.'

Sarah nodded, resigned to the facts. 'I wish you'd take my fucking husband instead, but he's worthless!' She slowly closed the door.

Later on Sarah perched herself on the side of Poppy's bed as she stroked her daughters hair. Both their faces were red from crying.

'Why can't they take dad's stuff?' There was anger in Poppy's voice as she spoke.

'Your dad-' Sarah stopped herself mid sigh. 'Sometimes, sweetie life isn't fair. Your dad had good intentions when he bought you the computer, but unfortunately good intentions aren't enough.' Sarah's voice was hollow and distant. 'Good intentions aren't good enough' she repeated and kissed Poppy on the forehead. As she pulled the duvet up to her daughter's chin. 'Try and get some sleep.'

Giles was in the kitchen washing the dishes as a peace offering when Sarah came downstairs. 'Is she ok?' He asked without looking away from the pan he was scrubbing.

'What do you think? She's just witnessed three men come and take her most prized possession away from her.' Sarah didn't even try and hide her contempt this time. She didn't mind sitting into the small hours trying to balance books that were becoming increasingly one-sided, she didn't mind scrimping and saving, shopping at the discounters, she didn't like the girls working more that they had to, but needs must. This time however he'd gone too far. Poppy, she was the reason Sarah did any of this. So that she wasn't affected. So that she didn't grow up knowing that they had no money. No matter how hard she tried to protect her she'd failed. Giles had lied and lied again and now her daughter was crying herself to sleep over a damn computer.

'I'm going to bed. Don't bother following me. You can sleep with the dogs tonight for all I care.' She grabbed a magazine from the kitchen table as she went to leave.

'Oh don't be so dramatic Sarah. I did a nice thing that didn't work out. She'll get over it and we'll get her a new computer in a month or two' Giles set the pot down and turned to face his wife, defiant. Sarah stopped in her tracks.

'You really don't get it, do you? Your mummy and daddy aren't here to bail you out anymore Giles. No, you pissed that trust fund away with your so called solid investments. No Giles, it's just us now and our pitiful income trying to maintain this, this, whatever this place is.' She threw her arms wide gesturing to the kitchen, 'It's not a house, it's sure as hell not a home. It's a noose. That's what it is, a fucking noose. We can barely see the end of each month, the debt letters keep piling up but you wouldn't know anything about those because you're too busy down the pub betting on horses you know nothing about. The Land Rover needs a service that we can't afford, we've had to cut Peter's hours so god knows if he'll stay with us. But you know what Giles, you're right everything's just fine. We'll get Poppy, Poppy by the way that's what our daughter is called. Poppy. Her name is Poppy. To signify hope. God I'm so naive. We'll get Poppy a new computer and everything will be hunky dory. Well you can get a computer and shove it up your arse because you have no idea. No idea what I have to do to stop us from sleeping in the streets. To stop Poppy living in a sleeping bag. God, I can't even look at you right now.' Sarah turned on her heels and left the kitchen her arms in mid air holding back her frustration. Giles stood motionless at the sink for a moment and then returned his attention to the pot he'd left to air dry a moment or two ago.

Not everything is free

Tatyana gazed in amazement at the women around her. They picked through clothes so absentmindedly. They missed the hard work that was poured into each garment as they passed. They didn't appreciate the work that had gone into making the clothes. Tatyana did, her hands felt every stitch, her fingers traced the lines of fabric as she stood in the store. She hadn't had new clothes in almost a year. Sarah had been so kind, she brought her here to go shopping. To begin her new life. Every girl deserves to feel pretty she'd told her this morning over breakfast. Tatyana had forgotten what it felt like to have someone notice her and make a fuss of her. It had been so long that anyone had made her feel like a girl let alone say she deserved anything. Other than what they desired for her.

Tatyana was excited to be shopping. She just couldn't make up her mind what to get. Sarah came over to her with a collection of items draped over her arm.

'See anything nice?' She asked with a smile.

'It's all so lovely. I don't know. Maybe this?' Tatyana asked for reassurance as she held up a black ribbed polo neck.

'Mmmm, I like it. That would go really well with some jeans.' Sarah held the top up against Tatyana's body. 'Let's go try some things on and see what you think. We can't buy everything but you definitely need a new wardrobe so best to get what you really like. You'll be most comfortable then. Bring that with you'. Sarah headed towards the changing rooms with her bundle and Tatyana in tow.

An hour and a half later Tatyana had picked out the black ribbed polo neck and a pair of light denim high waisted jeans. An off pink wool cardigan with three large buttons, a plain white t-shirt to go underneath and black cords. Alongside these she had a mixture of t-shirts, leggings and one navy sweatshirt. She had discarded the rest. Tatyana had never bought so many clothes at one time. Her smile had become a permanent fixture on her face as she paraded between the changing room and the seat that Sarah had sat on to provide expert commentary. Tatyana imagined she was a movie star as she and Sarah laughed when a dress or top looked terrible or when Sarah's eyes lit up as something really suited her. This must be what it's like to be normal. She had decided her favourite outfit and couldn't wait to go home and wear it properly. She was twisting in the changing cubicle her head looking back over her shoulder to make sure she'd seen every conceivable angle when Sarah knocked on the door.

'Tatyana, sweetie. One last item I'd like you to try on. We have a party coming up and I'd like you to wear it. Is that ok?'

'OK. Sure.' Tatyana opened the door and Sarah passed a tiny black mini skirt through the gap. 'It looks small.' Tatyana commented as she closed the door again to change.

'Can you try it on and let me see. We might have to get a bigger size then, but try that one on first sweetie.'

The smile that had rested so easily five minutes ago had gone from Tatyana's face as she opened the door to show Sarah the skirt. This time she didn't leave the cubicle. She stood there in the shadow of the door, barely covering herself as Sarah pulled her attention from her mobile phone and looked her up and down.

'Turn round so I can see sweetie.'

Tatyana pulled at the skirt so that it would cover her bum, but even with her holding it down with both hands the skirt didn't have the capacity.

'I think I need a bigger size' Tatyana spoke quietly, all her confidence from earlier had disappeared in the length of time it took to put on a skirt.

'No, that's perfect. Now come on. We have to go.' Sarah's demeanour had changed. The blossoming friendship they had just a few moments ago had gone, she was cold and detached as she spoke. There was a finality about her voice that Tatyana hadn't heard before from Sarah. Tatyana closed the door of the cubicle as Sarah turned to separate the clothes they were buying from the ones they weren't. 'I wish I knew a better way, I'm sorry'. Sarah whispered to the door of the cubicle.

Giles and Peter stood in the courtyard of the manor feeding the dogs. Giles enjoyed this time of the day. Dogs were loyal, simple. They didn't question your decisions. They didn't ask you about money, about the future. Just show up with food and they loved you.

Simple.

'I need you to do a favour for me Peter.' Giles didn't raise his head from pouring the meal into several tin feeding bowls as the dogs barked around his ankles.

'What do you need boss?' Peter's words were muffled as he was trying to light a cigarette he'd pulled from the side pocket of the black combat trousers he wore religiously.

'There's a cop I need you to tell to back off. Politely, but firmly. He's the husband of the woman I knocked down. I'm pretty sure he'll be coming after me and I need him to know that I'm not a pushover.'

'You mean he's the husband of the pregnant woman you killed?' Peter corrected Giles' version of the story.

Giles spun on his heels and squared up to Peter's chin, fury in his eyes. 'The woman I *accidentally* knocked down.'

Peter didn't flinch. He calmly exhaled his cigarette smoke into Giles' face. Giles' anger flamed like the end of Peter's cigarette. He shot back 'The reason you are here, may I remind you is to work for me' he stood more upright bringing his eye-line to Peter's forehead confident he'd reasserted his imagined authority.

Peter stood rooted to the spot. He inhaled another drag of his cigarette calming his thoughts. Any other time and he would have taught Giles a very painful lesson. But he was too close. Not yet.

'You've no idea why I'm here or who I'm after' Peter spoke through the smoke he'd directed upwards into Giles' nostrils. Visibly taken aback Giles struggled for words.

'Do as I say or I'll fire you quicker than you can finish that god awful cigarette!'

'Whatever you say, *boss*' Giles backed away as Peter held his ground. 'And if he doesn't take the hint?' Peter continued with his cigarette.

'We'll cross that bridge if necessary. But you can every persuasive if you want to be Peter. Make sure you are this time.'

Peter didn't respond. He shoved his hands into his pockets and walked away, his cigarette end glowing leaving Giles on his own to clear up after the dogs.

Sarah and Tatyana were waiting in the line to pay for the clothes. Neither of them spoke and Tatyana's shoulders had begun to slump. Sarah tried to break the ice. 'You've picked out some lovely outfits'. Tatyana just looked straight ahead ignoring the comment. Her mind was racing. Should she run? She didn't know anyone to run to or even where she was for that matter. She had no-one. Her only friend was Sarah. Was she a friend? Tatyana had thought so, now she wasn't so sure.

Paperwork

The windows in the conservatory of Officer Tony Knowles' home amplified the low winter sun making inside feel like a summers day. Tony sat in his favourite chair half interested in the book he was reading. Truth be told the book held as much interest as an electric bill. He closed the cover and took off the reading glasses he still wasn't accustomed to wearing. He rubbed the bridge of his nose and gently massaged his eyes, he didn't turn fifty for another eighteen months but he felt much older. The last few years had turned their life upside down and the stress was overwhelming at times. Moments of this tranquility were so infrequent he closed his eyes and sucked in a breath allowing his body to feel as much of it as he could.

Melissa, his fourteen year old sat on the sofa beside him engrossed with her phone. Their dog Hank readjusted himself as he lay on the floor at his feet. Tony was genuinely happy today. The news the family had been waiting for had finally arrived. Melissa had been accepted for pioneering treatment in Ohio. They had received the phonecall unexpectedly last week. When they had hung up the conversation had turned Melissa's inoperable brain tumour into hope. Not a lot but enough for the family to hold on to. That's all they asked for now. It had allowed them this day, to sit with their thoughts. The cancer was still in them just not shouting as loudly.

Melissa would be getting tired soon and she'd go back to bed for the rest of the day, but now he just enjoyed her company. He turned to watch her. To enjoy her. If it wasn't for her bald head she was a typical teenager, absorbed in whatever she was looking at online, it felt as though this is what a normal family day should be like. Today he didn't feel completely powerless. He treasured it. There were no nurses were stealing his time away from her. She wasn't lying in bed scared and crying asking questions he couldn't answer.

Tony didn't hear Remi knock on the front door and it was only when his wife Grace brought him in to the conservatory was he aware that they had company. Instantly he was annoyed at Remi for intruding. Remi could feel he'd encroached by being there.

'Sorry for interrupting' Remi was genuinely apologetic and not really sure why he was there in the first place.

Tony didn't answer, he was doing his best to hold on to the moments that had just lapsed, but they were like water trickling through his grasp.

'Don't be silly.' Grace dismissed any social impropriety thankful for someone to have a normal conversation with. 'Can I get you some tea?' she asked while motioning for Remi to take a seat.

'Uh, please, only if you're making one for yourself.'

'I am and I'm sure Tony would take one as well. Mel, honey, not much longer on that computer, your eyes will get tired.' Melissa made a noise from behind her screen and then as if her mum had reminded her to be tired she put her phone down.

'Think I'll go for a nap dad.'

'OK, sweetheart, love you'

'Love you too' she kissed his cheek as she moved past his chair and he closed his eyes to savour everything about the moment. Remi sat unseen, his grief choking his throat as he quietly mourned a memory he would never have.

When Tony opened his eyes again it was just him and Remi in the room as Hank had followed Melissa up to bed.

'Remi, to what do I owe the pleasure?'

'I'm sorry for coming to your house Tony, I am. You have a lovely family and I don't want to take time from you but this couldn't wait and I wasn't sure when you were back in the station.'

'Must be important'

'It is. I'm not sure if you're up to speed with any of the news, but do you know there was a woman knocked down three days ago. She died in hospital a short time later.'

'I heard. Apparently she was the wife of a policeman.' Tony's reply was half absent as Grace had returned with a tray of tea and biscuits.

'The woman was Laura, my wife, and she was carrying our unborn child.' Remi spoke matter of factly. It was all he could do.

The mugs of tea rattled as Grace could not contain her shock. She set the tray down. 'Dear God Remi. That's horrible. I'm so so sorry!'

Tony now shifted in his seat and gave his full

attention. 'Yes, I am very sorry for your loss Remi. How are you doing?' Tony was genuine.

'Honestly, I'm not sure Tone. It's all a bit of a bad dream at the minute. One that I just want to wake up from.' Remi sipped his tea as he spoke. He was more honest with these relative strangers than he had been with Louise.

'I get that. It's like you aren't quite here. As though you're absent from life.' Tony's words spoke of his experience.

Grace nodded in agreement. 'As if there's a barrier between you and,' she hesitated searching for the right word. It came, 'feeling.'

All three allowed their individual pain to form a quiet bond. Their lives intersecting at junctions none of them could have ever imagined.

'What do you need from us?' Tony set his mug down reached his hand over to hold his wife's.

Remi reached forward and took a digestive along with his tea. He explained to Tony and Grace what happened in as much detail as he could bare. He explained the charges against Giles and how they had been reduced, seemingly overnight.

'To be honest, it sounds as if there is something going on behind it.' Tony started to realise why Remi was sitting in his conservatory as he spoke. 'I hope you're not here to accuse me of anything, are you Remi?' He instinctively let go of Grace's hand.

'No. Not at all Tony. We haven't worked together but by all accounts you're not the type. I'm here to ask if you can remember anything, no matter what it is, anything you can think of that might help?'

'What you're saying makes sense' Tony became less

defensive. He stood up and leaned against the window to stretch his legs. 'I was just on shift, maybe an hour or so when I get a visit from an assistant at Reinholdt's office with the new paperwork forms. He explained that the paperwork had changed. The woman was an officer's wife so they wanted to be whiter than white. It was my first day back so I assumed I'd missed an update or memo or something. So, I filed the paperwork he gave me. I didn't think too much of it at the time. You know yourself how often new forms come down the chain.'

'What'd the guy look like?'

'He was bald, five nine-ish. Stocky. He had a few days stubble growth but not much else distinguishable. He didn't wear a suit, but passable office attire, I assumed he was working late and on his way home or something.'

'He said he'd come from Reinholdt's office?'

'Yeah.'

'The paper he gave you, do you have a copy or anything?'

'There's spares, he gave me a pile, I presume to appear more legitimate. I put them in the paperwork cupboard and threw out the old forms, or what I thought were the old forms. There should be a stack still there. Did you check?'

'To be honest no. I kinda flew off the handle and Bradley pulled me into his office. I came straight here.'

There was a loud clatter upstairs. Grace ran. A few seconds later she was calling for Tony.

'I'll let myself out, go.'

Tony nodded and left. Remi picked up the cups and left them into the kitchen before he left the Knowles family to their own pain.

A bent judge

Judge Theodore Reinholdt eased his portly body into his favoured armchair. He always chose the same chair when he visited the Marsden's. The brown leather arms framed him in and made him sit up taller than he normally did giving him an air of command in a house that wasn't his. Everywhere he went Theodore Reinholdt did his best to subtly increase his already formidable power. He saw that Sarah had already left an ashtray for him at the side table so took it as an invitation to fill his pipe.

'Sorry for keeping you waiting Judge' Sarah spoke on the half turn as she entered the room using her back to open the door. Her hands were full with a tray consisting of a pot of coffee for two and one glass of whiskey to wash it down.

'Nonsense. And please, call me Teddy. You know I prefer friends call me that.' He didn't. Privately Theodore despised the nickname Teddy. It was beneath him. It made him sound like some back alley crooner desperate for a break. Theodore commanded respect, Teddy smoked roll ups and had faded tattoos.

It had been his uncle who had taught him many years

ago the pleasure in manipulating those around you. Leon Reinholdt used the corner booth of his local bar as his pulpit and in young Theodore he found a willing audience.

'You'd be surprised how much faith people put into others Theodore. Most of us walk through our lives looking for a connection. To something, someone, anything. Give them that connection and you'll have a hold on them they'll want to keep.' He had just turned sixteen and his uncle had taken him to the bar for a drink to celebrate. Back then age restrictions around drinking were viewed more as suggestions. Theodore winced as he took a swig of whiskey inhaling his uncles words as well as his tobacco. 'The key is...' his uncle paused to take another draw of his cigarette. 'The key is to make the connection one way. Give them something that makes them feel special but to you is meaningless.' Theodore instantly understood and Teddy was born. The now grown Theodore brought his pipe to his nose and took a deep breath. The smell reminding him of time spent with his favoured uncle.

'Of course. Teddy. Please make yourself at home. To what do we owe the pleasure? This isn't a scheduled visit.' Sarah hid the concern rising inside her.

Teddy Reinholdt gestured for Sarah to sit in the chair opposite him as he lit his pipe with a practised flick of a match. It was Sarah's house but he had taken control of the room.

'No Sarah, unscheduled but I hope productive nonetheless.' Sarah waited silently. Reinholdt spoke like this with long pauses in his sentences. He liked making people wait for him. Sarah knew what he was doing and allowed him the space to preen. People like

Reinholdt had an inflated view of their own self importance. The key to getting them on your side was to let them inflate it themselves. 'I thought I should come and see you personally instead of sending a message.' He took a long draw on his pipe, savouring the taste before continuing. 'Given your husband's recent difficulties I thought it prudent that I stay away from your fundraiser this weekend.'

Sarah sighed. She had expected this. Reinholdt was a creep and a pervert but he had money, lots of it. One donation from him alone could run the manor for half a year. Giles had really thrown a spanner in the works this time. She couldn't blame Reinholdt. He was smart and it was the right thing to do. It just didn't suit her. Him not coming was bad, but if he took his friends with him it would be a complete disaster. Sarah needed to press him.

'I understand. My husband does have his difficulties I know.' her practiced laugh was almost sincere. 'I understand how this can put you in a poor position Teddy.' Sarah stood up and went to the door. She held the door open. 'I do appreciate you taking the time out of your very busy schedule to tell me yourself. I really do, it makes me glad we are friends Teddy, but I wouldn't want to take up any more of your time. After all I would hate a journalist to find out that you were visiting here. Giles has a bit of a profile these days with the local rags. Unfortunate really. Thankfully it's just the local papers I doubt they would catch on to your many visits over the last few years.' She held his gaze as she spoke, directly challenging him.

Fury sparked in Reinholdt's eyes. The composure that he was famous for was about to slip. His eyes darted around the room looking for something missing, something he hadn't spotted previously. Was he being framed? He stood as quickly as he could get out of the armchair he had nestled into. She had him. They both knew it.

'Don't panic Teddy.' Sarah closed the door and stood as close to him as his belly would allow. She whispered in his ear as she gently eased him back into the chair. 'I'm sure we can work out a way for you to continue supporting a cause that is so close to your heart.'

'I suppose I don't have to attend to donate.' He was on the backfoot.

'Really? Go on.' She eased him gently back into his chair as she caressed his shoulder and gently pecked his cheek. Her touch was too old for his tastes but it was always welcome.

Thirty minutes later Sarah had managed to extract the largest single payment she had ever received from Reinholdt with a promise of more to come. He had also committed the attendance of his wife and her girlfriends to the fundraiser. That was the good news. The bad news was she had changed the game. She was now blackmailing a judge. This wasn't what she wanted but she was losing control and this was what came to her in the moment.

Their relationship had changed and she could no longer rely on Reinholdt to help her in the future. She could see him plotting his escape and revenge even as they spoke. The politeness of his diction as they negotiated masked the betrayal that had taken hold of his ego and punctured it. It lay inside him wrinkled. This was his fault. He had forgotten the golden rule his uncle had told him. 'All power has an expiry date. If you don't control that, then your power wasn't real.' He had let himself enjoy the fruits of their relationship too much and now he was exposed.

Sarah's time was now limited and she didn't have a plan for what happened next. She would need to get one and quickly.

'If you'll excuse me just a moment I'll be right back.' Sarah smiled and picked up the tray and cleared the mugs away. 'Can I get you a refill?'

Reinholdt said nothing, he'd said enough. He tapped his glass to indicate a top up of whiskey. His polite smile barely caged the rage he felt inside. He was two years from mandatory retirement and he could not afford to pay the Marsdens what he had just promised them. He had been stupid and hadn't protected himself from the start. Now he was in trouble. He had bought some time, but not much. He needed help. He needed to enlist the help of Tony or Monty, or both? He wasn't sure yet. What he was sure of however was that Sarah Marsden had just made a very powerful enemy.

A minute later Sarah came back into the room with a young girl. This piqued his attention. She was new. 'Teddy, this is Tatyana. She has just come to us for a while.' Tatyana stood awkwardly in the room holding a bottle of whiskey in her hand. She wore the skirt Sarah had made her buy yesterday. 'Tatyana sweetie, I'm sure Teddy would like another glass of whiskey.' Her hand rested on Tatyana's lower back and she gently pushed her further into the room. 'I'll let you two get to know each other. Teddy here is a very special friend of Mama's so I want you to be good to him, for me.' Sarah smiled and looked directly at Teddy as she spoke. She closed the door as Tatyana stood in the middle of the room looking for someone to save her.

Never one to look a gift horse in the mouth Theodore Reinholdt made himself comfortable again. *I can deal with her betrayal later. Might as well enjoy this young lady while I can.* He raised his empty glass and patted the seat that Sarah had just vacated.

Mystery man

Remi shifted uncomfortably in a single chair in the air conditioned foyer of Mason & Jones law firm. Large floor to ceiling glass windows made air conditioning a necessity even in Ireland. After waiting patiently for the last thirty minutes he decided to give his back a rest and went to look out the windows that overlooked the centre of Belfast. As he watched the rhythm of the city his attention was pulled to different scenes. Two young girls laughed at a bus-stop as they shared the screen of a phone. An older couple sat at the window of a coffee shop blissfully in silence, company more important than communication. A middle aged man reading a folded newspaper. Each of them unaware they had provided a brief cameo in Remi's day.

He was waiting to see one of the legal secretaries about the paperwork that had been filed for the Giles Marsden case. He wasn't sure what he was looking for but it sure as hell beat sitting at home alone avoiding all the jobs that he knew he'd have to do at some point. Simple things, like the washing. The basket was filled. Her clothes would still be in it. The day to day routine hadn't caught up with her death yet.

The receptionist came over to offer him a top up and

apologise yet again for the delay pulling him to the present.

'I'm sorry for the delay sir, you know lawyers. Meetings always running over. Can I offer you a top up?

Remi turned from the window.

'No, thank you. I'm fine.' He was beginning to get restless and decided to try a punt. 'I'll be sure to make an appointment the next time. Tell me, how long have you been working here…Sharon?' her name tag was helpful.

'Thirty seven years this year.' Unconsciously she stood up straighter as she spoke, happy for once to be noticed. 'I'm more qualified than half the lawyers in here.'

'Thirty seven years? now you're lying!' Remi was genuinely surprised. People didn't stay in jobs for that long these days. He was useless at guessing ages and as far as he could tell Sharon could have ranged anywhere between late forties and mid sixties. Yellowing around her fingers pointed to a cigarette habit, but he felt there was an inner peace about the woman standing in front of him now. *Maybe she stopped ageing when she found it?*

'You must have started here young. How come you didn't move across to the court room? Meetings too long?' Remi smiled as he worked his charm. He had an effortless ease about him that allowed people to warm to him, today he needed to remember where to find it.

'I started here when I was twenty one. The plan was to get my degree and have a wonderful career. Then I fell in love and got pregnant. My wonderful boy. He has special needs and it was more important for me to be there for him. So I stayed in the front office' There was a complete absence of regret in her words. It had been the right decision for her and she was very comfortable in that. Her peace was shining. 'He's a lucky boy. I'm sure that was tough.'

'Do you have a family? I can't imagine a handsome young man like you doesn't?'

Remi hesitated not knowing how to answer. Did he have a family anymore? Laura and bump lived in his heart. They plagued his thoughts, all the time. But like the people on the other side of the window he couldn't touch them. Where did that leave him?

'It's complicated.' He forced a smile.

'Family is.' Sharon spoke with a knowing wisdom only age can bring. 'Well, I'll not pry, but if you'll take any advice, you hold on to them as long as you can. Take it from me, it goes by in the blink of an eye.' There was a pause and Sharon moved on. 'You sure I can't get you a top up?'

'No thanks.' Remi became distant, the conversation hadn't gone where he'd wanted it to. He'd hoped to probe into the firm, not his personal life. He wasn't ready for this.

'Maybe I'll come back another time. Make an appointment.'

'OK then. If you want, but I'm sure one of these young hotshots will be along any time soon. You've waited long enough already.'

'I wouldn't say hotshots Sharon'. Richard Young held out his hand to greet Remi as he walked across the foyer. His blue suit was tight and immaculate, matched with polished brown brogues. He didn't wear the matching jacket instead a waistcoat allowed him to show a developed physique underneath a pressed white shirt. Remi guessed Richard was in his early twenties, he was much easier to guess than Sharon. Life hadn't hit him yet.

'Richard Young, I'm one of the legal secretaries here at Mason & Jones. I'm sorry to have kept you officer...'

'Wallace. Remi Wallace.' He'd missed his chance to leave. He was now committed. 'I was wondering if you could answer a couple of questions around the procedure in one of Judge Reinholdt's recent cases.' Remi showed his badge, thankful for the change of subject.

'Of course officer. Please follow me. Did Sharon get you coffee ok? She makes the best coffee.' Either it was a rhetorical question or Richard Young had forgotten he'd asked it because he was still talking away to himself along the corridor as Remi turned back to say thank you to Sharon. She smiled and rolled her eyes as the young legal secretary could still be heard in the distance.

Exactly thirty seven minutes later Remi was back in the foyer thanking Richard for his time. The meeting had been useless. Typical lawyer. Evasive and feigning help. Remi couldn't put his finger on it but something didn't feel right about the whole thing. He wanted to speak to Sharon again. He checked the reception desk to see if she was still there, she wasn't. A young girl in oversized glasses now sat in her place heavily engrossed in her work, typing at the computer.

'Excuse me' Remi interrupted

'Yes Sir. How can I help?' The young girl instantly

stopped her typing and smiled.

'Has Sharon finished for the day? She was here earlier I just wanted to say goodbye'

'She's on her lunch. She'll be back at two. Or if you're lucky you'll catch her having a smoke in the staff carpark at the back.'

'A woman after my own heart' Remi lied and made his way to the carpark. It would be worth waiting around for a bit to see if Sharon knew anything Richard wasn't prepared to divulge. A quiet carpark would be perfect.

He was in luck. Tucked in a doorway shielding herself from the light rain that patted the windscreens of the cars left in the carpark Sharon was enjoying the last couple of drags of her cigarette in peace.

'Mind if I join you?'

Sharon raised an eyebrow. 'Sure thing. I never say no company. All these young ones are far too healthy so I'm here on my own most of the time. You get what you wanted?' she asked as she pulled out a packet of cigarettes for Remi to share. He declined.

'I don't smoke.'

'And you sure as hell don't want to take me for dinner.' She put the packet back in her coat pocket. 'So I'm guessing you didn't find young Mr Young all that helpful, officer.'

'The problem is I don't really know what it is that I'm looking for, so I don't know if he was helpful or not. I was wondering if you could maybe help? I'm guessing you know more about the people who come and go in this office?'

'I'd say I do. But that doesn't mean much.' Sharon took a long drag on her cigarette silently offering Remi to ask his questions.

'I'm working on a case that went to Judge Reinholdt. The client Giles Marsden was represented by this law firm.' Sharon exhaled a cloud of nicotine as Remi spoke. 'The thing is, Mr Marsden received a laughable sentence.' Remi remained as professional as he could unsure whether it would help him or not to let Sharon know his connection. 'In addition wrong paperwork was filed by the police which doesn't add up to me. This kind of stuff happens all the time. But I'm not so sure about this, it doesn't feel right. I've spoken to the police officer who submitted the paperwork and he says a lawyer from here gave him what they said was updated paperwork to submit.' Sharon remained silent so Remi continued. 'The lawyer, male, late 40's to mid 50's with shaved head. Well built. You know of anyone who works here or you've seen around here who matches that description?'

Sharon took another drag of her cigarette assessing in her head her options. 'I know the case, but why are you so interested in this case? You said it yourself, paperwork, either incomplete or incorrect gets filed regularly. Light sentences are a daily occurrence, in over thirty years in this firm you're the first policeman who has ever come and followed up on a light sentence.'

'New protocol.' Remi lied and instantly regretted it. She would see right through him.

'Bullshit.' Sharon stubbed what remained of her cigarette out and went to go past him.

'Alright. I'm sorry. I shouldn't have said that.' He put his arm out to stop her going past. 'It's just the truth is too raw at the minute'

Sharon stopped in her steps and looked at Remi. She saw his pain and understood. 'You knew the girl.' Remi held up his left hand with his wedding ring still on it in response. He couldn't return her look.

'Dear god sweetie. I'm so sorry.' Sharon placed a motherly hand on his shoulder. 'There isn't much I can tell you I'm afraid. But maybe I can point you somewhere. Firstly there isn't anyone who works here with that description but that doesn't surprise me either.'

'How come?'

Sharon checked her watch and pulled out her cigarettes to light another. 'I've only got a couple of minutes so listen up.' She placed the cigarette in her mouth and two flicks of her lighter had the tobacco glowing. 'This firm is called Mason & Jones. But it wasn't always. When I started here it was called Reinholdt & Partners. Your Judge Reinholdt was the founder. Now as a judge you aren't able to be a partner in a law firm or have any dealings with a law firm. It clouds your impartiality.'

'Makes sense.'

'Sure it does. On paper. But you think these judges are going to cut ties with all the people they have spent years working with? Of course not. They're people. They have relationships they've built up over the years just like you or me.'

'Go on'. Remi could feel his mind ready to jump, it just didn't know where. Sharon could see it in his face.

'Reinholdt's former founding partner Marty Mason, he might be the missing link. He doesn't practice any more, he spends most of his days on the golf course. But every Saturday morning he and Reinholdt form a fourball. They have done for years.'

'Marty Mason?   As in the business man Marty Mason?' Remi asked

'One and the same.   Marty was a partner here very early on and then he moved across to the business world.   But he kept a silent partnership here.   The description of the guy you gave doesn't fit the type here, but it could be any one of the the bodyguards Marty employs to keep him and his family safe'.

'So Reinholdt got Marty to change the paperwork for the case? Why would he do that?'

'Maybe he did.   Maybe he didn't.   I'm not saying either way. What I am saying though is your Judge has a relationship to this firm even if he technically doesn't. Now that doesn't mean he's done anything wrong. Incorrect paperwork gets filed all the time.   You know that.   If you're going to go around making accusations about Judges changing paperwork you'd have to have much more to go on than a weekly fourball with an old partner that doesn't even practice law anymore.   He would get fired and possibly face jail time.   What motivation would someone a year or two from retirement and a Judge's pension possibly have to jeopardise all that?   Not to mention Marty Mason, the one thing he doesn't need is money.'

Remi stood in silence processing what Sharon has just told him.

'I hope you get sorted sweetheart, I really do.   I'm sorry for what you're going through, truly I am.   But I'm not sure there's much else I can tell you and I need to get back to the office.'

'Yeah, thanks. I appreciate it Sharon.'

'Would you take a piece of advice from an old

woman?'

'Sure.'

'When you're done with this learn how to make peace with it all and yourself. Your pain, it's helping you now but it will eat you apart quicker than cancer given half the chance.'

Same old story

'Please my dear, have a seat.' Reinholdt's eyes devoured all of Tatyana's body but they lingered on her not quite developed breasts. Tatyana twisted trying to protect herself from his hungry gaze, her feet rooted to the spot. She fought back tears as her lips winced a smile.

'Come. Tatyana was it? I'm Theodore, but my good friends call me Teddy. I'd like you and I to become good friends,' he gestured towards a pouffe that he pulled towards his armchair. Tatyana couldn't move. She didn't want to let Sarah down, but she knew what was coming. Her body wouldn't let her, as though her feet were nailed to the carpet.

'Come now. You wouldn't want mama's guest to go thirsty now, would you?' he raised his crystal tumbler that still had more than one measure in it to add a some theatrics to the question. Tatyana didn't reply. The clinking of the ice cubes released her from her frozen state and she slowly sat on the edge of the pouffe furthest away from the armchair and topped up the judge's glass.

'Thank you' Reinholdt indicated that his glass was now full enough and she placed the bottle on the table beside a ceramic reading lamp within touching distance. She made herself as hidden and as small as she could. Her knees remained together, angled away from the judge, eyes focussed on the floor just in front of her toes and her right arm cradled her left elbow across her lap.

Reinholdt shifted forward in his chair. He reached his hand out and began to gently stroke her hair. She pulled her shoulder up and head down trying to block him. She fought this reaction knowing she would disappoint Sarah and slowly released the tension on her right side. Reinholdt was pleased and continued to run his fingers gently through her hair

'Tell me about yourself, where do you come from?' He became bolder and let his fingers trace the side of her cheek and down her neckline.

Instinctively Tatyana shrugged her shoulder to knock his hand out of the way.

That was it. Reinholdt had had enough of women not showing him the respect he deserved today. Particularly this little bitch. He slammed his glass on the side table, grabbed Tatyana by both shoulders turning her to face him and pulling her close at the same time. His reaction and force frightened her and she arched back trying to keep some distance. This enraged Reinholdt further. He lunged towards her trying to kiss her mouth with his. Tatyana seized up at the sight of this red face and bulging eyes attacking her. She pulled back even harder, memories of her brothers and their friends came flooding back to her. Reinholdt pulled her tighter, his hands gripped her arms trying to hold them to her side. It didn't work. Tatyana had become rigid. She hadn't come all the way here to have this fat bastard use her like everyone else. Her life started now. She used her legs and kicked backwards, Reinholdt's lunge missed her and he fell further forward. She freed her right hand which she used to slap Reinholdt hard across the face as he was sprawling over the pouffe. Reinholdt let her go as he reeled in pain and shock. Tatyana knocked the table and side lamp over as she stood and got herself free.

Reinholdt remained on his knees holding his cheek in disbelief. Tatyana stood over him readying herself for the reprisal. She knew what was coming and she was ready.

'Why you little-' Reinholdt went to grab her legs but Tatyana moved back and he missed. She stood just out of his reach, her breathing heavy. Her eyes scanned the room looking for something she could use as a weapon. She was isolated, Reinholdt was between her and the book shelves which held any number of volumes heavy enough to hurt.

Reinholdt regathered himself. He smiled as he stood wiping a drop of blood from the side of his mouth. They both stood staring at each other when Sarah entered. She'd heard the lamp break. Quickly assessing the situation Sarah focussed on the judge.

'Tatyana. Leave. Now.' Tatyana left the room without saying a word. Sarah's eyes didn't leave Reinholdt until she heard the door close behind her. He went to speak but Sarah cut him off. She was furious. 'I don't know what just happened here, and I don't want to. This is not some cheap brothel where you get to slap my girls about and think that's ok.'

'I'm the one with blood on my face Sarah'

'Unprovoked I'm sure.' She wasn't in the

mood.

Sarah began to clean up the lamp while Reinholdt dabbed at his lip with a tissue. Sarah needed to make a peace offering. First blackmail and now this. She handed him his glass.

'I'll speak with Tatyana. In the meantime perhaps it would be better if we started afresh. Maybe you'd be more comfortable with someone you already know. On the house of course.'

Reinholdt thought. He regretted coming here. Events hadn't gone the way he'd planned at all. However a girl on the house might not make it worthwhile but it would certainly dull the pain for a moment. 'Of course. That would be welcome.'

'Make yourself comfortable, and enjoy your drink. Do you need another tissue for your mouth?'

'No. I'm fine thank you.'

Sarah nodded in agreement and took the remnants of the lamp with her. She stopped as she reached the door. 'Teddy, I expect my all my girls to be treated well. You know this. I hope you don't feel the need to, how shall I put it, vent any frustrations?'

'My word as a gentleman.'

'I'll be back shortly.'

Reinholdt fumed over his whisky. He had known this day would come at some point. But he wasn't prepared enough. He'd let himself enjoy the services Sarah provided too much and now he was exposed. He'd have to let things lie for a week or two until he was able to mobilise his contingency. One thing was for certain. Judge Theodore Reinholdt was not about to be taken advantage of by this little bitch. He'd enjoy this afternoon and start to put plans in motion once he got back to his office.

A knock at the door interrupted his thoughts. Anna appeared wearing a skirt that redefined the term 'mini'. Her smile put him at ease and he sat back in his chair. He liked Anna. She respected him. He leaned his head back staring at the ceiling as Anna sank to her knees and unbuckled his belt. Yes. He would let himself enjoy this afternoon.

Peter's story

Peter stood staring at the notice board with the towel he'd used after his shower wrapped around his waist. The dagger tattoo on his chest had now started to fade and the ink had spread slightly but it was still instantly recognisable as the royal marine commando branding. He'd let his hair grow a little longer than he'd kept when in service but marine conditioning was now part of his DNA. At nearly fifty years old he was in great shape and exercised daily. Physical fitness had always come easily to him and he could still execute a hundred push ups at a moments notice.

The notice board was kept under the bed in the only bedroom of his tiny rented apartment. It was rare he had any visitors and even rarer anyone was in his bedroom. That didn't matter. He needed to minimise the risk. The board was filled with pictures of Giles, Sarah and Judge Theodore Reinholdt. Should any of them happen to call unexpectedly and see the board, all his work would be for nothing. He couldn't take the chance.

Along one side he had pinned the pictures that he had taken of children he had seen in his time working for the Marsdens. He knew they were linked but couldn't quite get close enough to land the telling blow. Until Tatyana. When she arrived he had helped Sarah pull her from the cell she kept in the outbuildings of the manor. This was the piece he had needed. Now he was close. He just needed to link the parts together.

The last few months had torn him apart. He knew young girls and boys were being exploited and he had to sit back and watch until he gathered proof. More than once he had to stop himself from killing them all. He couldn't, death would be too quick for them. Years ago he had made a promised to himself to make their pain last as long as possible. He knew how to administer pain, make it last.

He had come home for Reinholdt. But the web was larger than he had imagined. It involved more people than just Reinholdt. Only once he was sure he knew all the moving parts would he take action. Reinholdt was his. The rest of them he'd leave for the police.

He pulled a plastic bag containing two items that he carried with him everywhere from his black combat trousers lying on the bed. One was a photo of a young girl, she was nineteen at the time the photo was taken, smiling at the camera. It was only after his sister had committed suicide did Peter start to see the sadness in her eyes. It was a sadness that wasn't part of her. It had come to visit her and she hadn't been able to get it to leave. Her eyes haunted him every time he looked at his last photo of her.

The other item was a letter she had written to him while he had been stationed in Iraq. By the time he received it and had his leave approved it was too late. He arrived back in the UK to find her hanging in her bedroom from the night before. She was unable to carry the burden of shame she had felt.

Peter knew exactly why Samantha had killed herself. Her letter had told him. Although there was over ten years difference in age between them they had been extremely close. As close as they could be with Peter across the globe at a couple of days notice. He was her protector and he'd failed her. He wouldn't fail her again.

After her suicide Peter had another twelve years service to complete before he could gain his military pension. He returned to operations with a renewed vigour and deep seeded anger that allows you to make a name for yourself in the military. He quickly moved from an unassuming private with no real direction to the standout recruit. A new focus combined with his appetite for the most dangerous assignments had him quickly passing Royal Marine Commando selection ultimately becoming a mountain leader. He excelled during all missions, becoming the leader of his own unit, eventually being awarded the Distinguished Service Order for his command in the Afghan Central Highlands. His appetite for danger was borderline insatiable.

None of this work however eased the guilt that he felt over Samantha. He hadn't been there when she needed him most. By the time his twelve years were over the Marines couldn't persuade him to stay and he retired with honours and his full pension.

The steady income of his pension allowed him to focus on his new mission. Judge Theodore Reinholdt. It didn't take too long to track him down. In her letter Samantha only referred to him as Theo, and that he was working in the law firm that she was interning in during the summer. That was more than enough information for him to work with.

Now dried and wearing loose shorts and a t-shirt Peter sat down on the sofa with a beer to read the letter he had memorised, just in case there was anything he'd missed. There wouldn't be but his apartment had no TV and he wasn't great at socialising.

Hi Pete,

How's you? I miss you! I really hope you are enjoying army life. I hope it is as exciting as I think it is whenever I think about what you do. In my dreams I see you travelling to far off exotic places, overturning tyranny one week and rescuing villagers the next.

Things here are ok, I guess. The summer started well. I got my placement at Reinholdt and Mason's. They specialise in employment law, which is exactly what I want to do. I'll fight the directors, you fight the dictators, together bro we'll change the world!

It started off fine, standard stuff really. There are three interns, myself, Amy & Chris. We pretty much just do filing, take meeting minutes, make tea. Nothing thrilling. The other two moan about it constantly, they think we should be working on huge cases. I didn't mind, I was just happy to be here getting experience. I've always wanted to be a lawyer so it's cool just seeing how a firm actually works.

Three weeks ago I was asked by Theo to help on a larger scale project. He said he wanted me because he knew the other two complained about the work they'd been given and I didn't. It would mean longer hours and he hoped I didn't mind. I didn't. This is exactly what I wanted. More work and big projects.

From here though things got worse. I hope you don't mind me telling you, I just have nowhere to turn. I feel trapped. I know you can't help where you are but me writing it down feels like therapy.

In our first meeting Theo outlined the project and ordered in Chinese for the whole team. There was five of us in total, and I was by far the youngest. It was great, it felt just like all those old law movies I made you watch growing up. We were working late, planning the best strategy to win! Later that night when the others in the project team had gone home he asked me to hang around for a bit to make sure the paperwork was all correct for tomorrow. It was then he began to touch me. At first I brushed it off as an accident. But then he was more and more deliberate. There was no mistaking. I protested and he backed off. The next night he tried again. Again I said no. This time though he told me that he'd hoped I be more "helpful" in work and that he'd have to ask to get my internship cancelled. I need this for my course credits. It took two years to get this placement. If I get it cancelled I can't qualify.

The other interns have started talking and are more and more standoffish. I hear what they say, not to my face, but the whispers. They stop when I come into the room. They judge me relentlessly. I feel isolated. I spoke to my course tutor. He was useless. He told me to be very careful about what I say. Theo is a respected man in the community. Such allegations wouldn't help me in any way.

I called in sick for a couple of days but then my tutor phoned to say that if I didn't show up then he'd have to fail me. So for the last week I've let him have sex with me. It's gross. I'm gross. We work late, but what this means is we work for about an hour and then he starts to come on to me and then we end up having sex in the conference room. After we're done, he makes us carry on with the work.

I hate it. I hate myself but I don't know where to turn. I need this job, it's only for another two months. I know it's not rape because technically I let him, but somehow this feels worse. I am completely helpless. I just wish there was a way out. I wish I could just sit on the sofa and watch a crappy movie with you and feel safe. Just like we used to.

I'm so sorry I've let you down. I wish I was as strong as you. I'm sorry. I'm sorry for rambling.

Sam xx

Her letter had underplayed who he was. Peter thought he was just some junior associate taking advantage of her. He wasn't. It turned out that Theo was a founding partner of Reinholdt and Mason's a firm he and his partner had set up straight out of university. Initially they had noble intentions working to help individuals with employment rights. But that moved quickly into compensation claims, it turns out that was more lucrative. Or easier. Probably both.

His years of training with the marines had made him an expert in recce missions and once he pinpointed Reinholdt Peter had bided his time and gathered as much intel as he could. After six months of stalking the judge he found nothing unusual in the Judge's routine. He worked hard and seemed to be professional in how he conducted himself. He spent long hours in the office which left little time for any real socialising or other hobbies. His marriage was traditional in the sense that his wife managed the household and she drove whatever social engagements he could commit to. He would occasionally decline the invite and blame work, instead choosing to watch TV on is own once his wife had left. He had a regular Saturday fourball followed by lunch at the club. As routine and monotonous as it sounded.

Throughout all of his reconnaissance Peter didn't see Theodore Reinholdt around one minor. Not one sniff of a relationship that could be construed as inappropriate. To all intents and purposes Judge Theodore Reinholdt was a model citizen. It was just that Peter knew otherwise.

There was one black spot. Since he had begun his mission Reinholdt had made three unscheduled visits to the Marsden's. His calendar was cleared and marked as a private appointment. These appointments were the only time he changed his schedule. Something didn't add up and it was clear he spent important time at the Marsdens who sat outside his normal social circle. He needed to get closer. Reconnaissance in plain sight.

The plan had been simple. Giles and Sarah had a handy man already working for them, Peter needed to relieve him from his duties. Some gentle persuasion over a pint and the previous handyman decided it was in his best interests to leave his employment with immediate effect. Some tampering with the land rover and ensuring he was in the right place at the right time and Peter very quickly became indispensable to the Marsdens. More than two hours with Giles and it was clear that he was not the type to do much around the house.

Initially Peter had felt sorry for Sarah. How wrong he was. He played the role well. Quiet, unassuming and observant. Very quickly he had found out that Sarah was the main orchestrator of trafficking. She used the girls and sometimes boys to help grease the wheels for the life she wanted. Giles was incompetent in most ways of life, Sarah effectively came behind and tidied up. She had most of the local influencers in her pocket from what he could gather going by the visitors who came and went to the manor house.

Once he'd finished his beer Peter carefully folded the letter along the creases and placed it back into the ziplock bag he had kept it in for years. The letter was in almost perfect condition despite being almost twenty years old. The ink was fading slightly and the bottom left corner had a tea stain when one of his unit knocked over a stove in Afghanistan. Peter had overreacted at the time. Three men pulled him off the cadet. His unit were all tired having marched for two nights straight on a recce mission based on poor information and Peter had let his frustrations boil over. It was the only time he'd used poor judgement.

He didn't allow himself the luxury of poor judgement this time. This was too important and the one mission he could not fail at. He kissed the photo of Samantha whispering "almost there" before placing the ziplock bag back in the pocket of his combat trousers.

Reinholdt pulls a favour

Marty Mason sat in his private bar of the golf club he owned waiting on the daily special to be brought over for lunch. He wasn't in a good mood. A bogey, bogey finish had capped off a terrible round. He would need to spend more time on the practice range tomorrow.

Retired long ago Marty struggled to get a game midweek with his peers, most of who still had to grind out a paycheque, so every Wednesday he played a round with some of his staff. For them it was a great opportunity to talk to the boss about what was happening in work. For Marty it was his way of keeping in touch without being in the office. In general the staff he played with were much younger than him and provided a good challenge. His playing partners today doubled up as his personal bodyguards. In all honesty he enjoyed these games more than his weekend fourballs which had become tiresome long ago.

The waiter brought over three house specials of Guinness pie and chips and a bottle of sparkling water. Marty started to tuck in when the phone in his pocket began to ring. He pulled it out and saw Reinholdt's personal number on the screen. He turned the tones off and put it back in his pocket. He despised Theodore

Reinholdt and his afternoon was bad enough as it was. Their relationship was based on leverage. Reinholdt had it and Marty didn't. It had been this way for far too long.

In his early twenties Marty had started work at Reinholdt's law firm. He was bright, worked hard and enjoyed the grey areas that law operated in. Very quickly his position allowed him to get the inside track on a number of businesses. He was then able to creatively gain control of the businesses that he felt showed promise. Young and focussed Marty flew up the ranks. He was ruthless with an uncanny ability to spin any argument. Reinholdt had made him partner after one year much to the disgust of more senior staff in the team, most of whom had left soon after in protest.

Three years after joining the firm Marty himself resigned. The businesses he had acquired allowed him to earn a substantial income freeing up the time he needed to work on his first passion. Golf.

The day he decided to retire is the day he found out that Reinholdt was more shrewd than he had ever given him credit for. Sitting in Reinholdt's office laid out in front of him was a map of exactly how Marty had acquired his extra income allowing him to be able to retire at such a young age. Reinholdt didn't say a word. Instead he sat back in his chair and took his time filling his pipe. He had him and the both knew it. Marty was facing a minimum of ten years in prison as well as his businesses stripped from him. At the time he had a young wife and family that needed him to support them. His options were low at best. Thankfully Reinholdt's offer was generous, at least that's what he thought.

Marty was to leave the firm, but retain partner status

and receive a nominal monthly stipend. In exchange Reinholdt would receive 15% of the monthly turnover of his businesses deposited into a private account. The figure Reinholdt had produced was close enough to the actual amount that Marty knew he wasn't bluffing. So Marty reluctantly agreed. For the last twenty years Reinholdt has received on average exactly the same amount of money every month, adjusted for inflation which now represented less than 1% of Marty's income. Not once has the amount been challenged. Money was never the motivator for Reinholdt. He coveted something much harder to come by; power and control.

For the duration of his lunch Marty Mason's phone buzzed in his pocket constantly. He refused to answer it, but like a fly on a summers night it became more and more irritating.

By the time he had finally cleared his plate and wiped his mouth with the cloth napkin he had 23 missed calls, every single one of them was from Theodore Reinholdt. It buzzed again. This time he picked up the phone and his minders started to stand and let him take the call in private. He gestured them to stay as he placed the phone at his ear.

'Theodore.' His tone flat and distant.

There were pauses in between him speaking in order to let Reinholdt talk.

'I know. I can see the missed calls. I was having my lunch. A lovely Guinness pie. I recommend you try it next time you're at the club.'

Pause

'Well, I've learnt that recently everything is urgent with you.'

Pause

'I see. The problem with that Teddy, is that if everything is urgent then nothing is.'

Pause

'That would be your issue, not mine.'

There was a long pause and Reinholdt's raised voice could be heard coming through the speaker.

'You're getting flustered Teddy. Now just take a breath and calm down.'

Pause.

'One minute.' Marty held his hand over the phone and turned to his minders. 'Gents, would you mind giving me a minute.' His bodyguards obliged and swiftly left the table. Once they were out of earshot Marty returned to his phonecall.

'Theo, these requests are becoming more and more frequent, wouldn't you say?'

Reinholdt responded with his normal bluster. 'You owe me!...' Marty tuned out of the conversation and set the phone down on the table, Reinholdt still ranting on the other end of the line. Marty took a deep breath, closed his eyes, rubbed his temples and thought.

'Hello? Marty? You still there?'

'I'm thinking. Shut up for a second.'

The pair of them sat in their own silence miles apart.

'I've come to a decision.' Marty picked up the phone so he didn't have to raise his voice. 'You've done extremely well out of me over the last twenty years. You had leverage over me and you made use of it. That, I must commend you for. In turn, I've made you a very rich man. I neither care nor do I want to know what you've done with the money, that is not my problem. You get this one favour and this is your last favour. I'll get Steve to follow and report. I'll see what he says and come back to you. He will only follow and report, he will not get involved. You are not bringing my men into whatever fucking mess you've got yourself into this time. Do you understand?'

'Yes. Of course.' Reinholdt assured him he understood, which of course he did. He didn't like it but he understood it.

Marty continued. 'Now listen carefully to this part. This is us even. I don't owe you anything else. We're done. You've used your leverage. You've been more than fairly compensated. I owe you nothing. You no longer have any dealings with me at all. You're even out of the Saturday fourball. Delete my number and never contact me again.'

He hung up and sat in silence. Reinholdt thought he was a tough guy, he wasn't. He enjoyed the finer things in life too much. Whiskey and girls, especially young girls were his weakness and always got him in some sort of trouble. Unfortunately for Marty, the real problem was that he never kept his troubles to himself. Over the last six months Reinholdt had began to shift the rules of the relationship pulling either Marty or his minders into the silly problems Reinholdt's dick got him into. Marty didn't like problems especially other peoples.

Reinholdt had become a significant problem. One that needed dealt with. He could kill him, but killing a sitting judge would give him even more headaches. Reinholdt will have to wait, for now.

Back to the start

Tatyana hacked at her hair with the brush. Her anger blocking her from making any real progress. With every stroke she hoped to erase a memory. The brush came to an abrupt halt as she found a knot that brute strength couldn't get through. She needed to calm down, take a breath and slowly disentangle the brush from her hair. That didn't happen. She pulled even harder, the pain stabbing at her head allowed her to feel the pain swirling inside her.

Sarah didn't knock as she came into the room. 'How could you do that to me Tatyana? After all I've done for you!' Her eyes bulged demanding answers.

Tatyana stopped mid-stroke and looked at Sarah scarcely able to believe what she had just heard.

'Done for me?' years of rage built up inside Tatyana became unleashed. She stood and stared down Sarah as she screamed in her face pointing the hairbrush in her chest. 'How could I so that to you? *You,* you were supposed to help me. *You* were supposed to save me from that. But no, you're worse.' Tatyana grew as she spoke. 'My brothers, my father, all hated me. But you. You were supposed to be my friend. You.' Tatyana made sure the hairbrush connected with Sarah's shoulder this time. Sarah took an involuntary step back. ' You. What are you gaining from me?'

Sarah froze. She knew that Tatyana was right but she couldn't accept it. *I'm a good woman. I help girls.* 'No, no, that's not true'. Her words rang hollow. Tatyana had seen her soul and it was black.

Tatyana began to unleash years of hurt. 'You're worse than anyone. You come to me like a friend yet you use me like a slave.' The venom of her words and fury of her screams ripped through Sarah and she squeezed past her needing to sit on the bed. Tatyana was now standing screaming in the room. Not just at Sarah but at the world.

'I am more than this. I am important and I have dreams. Fuck you Sarah. Fuck you!' Sarah remained motionless on the bed not daring to respond, Tatyana needed to let this out. With every word Tatyana found herself growing in strength. By voicing her anger she had found a confidence that was forgotten.

'You were supposed to protect me.' Tatyana took a moment to gather herself. Sarah saw her window.

'Tatyana, honey, you don't — '

'I don't what? Understand?' Tatyana glared at Sarah. Her eyes daring her to respond. Sarah backed down and sat motionless on the bed. Tatyana wasn't going to let her off the hook just yet.

'Well? What is it I don't understand? You owe me that at least.'

'It's…it's just…' Sarah searched for a word that wouldn't enflame the situation. '…complicated, that's all.'

'Complicated?' Tatyana folded her arms. 'How? Men pay you to fuck me. It doesn't seem that complicated to me.'

'That's not how it is.'

'Really? So what did you expect me to do downstairs? And what is Anna doing right now?'

Sarah rubbed her face with her hands.

'Anna...' Sarah trailed off. She knew how the words sounded even before she said them out loud.

'You're just a fucking fraud. You live here in your big house and loving family but all you are is a fraud'.

Sarah continued to rub her face. Tatyana was right. She was a fraud. This house, her marriage it was all a fraud.

Tatyana stood in the middle of the bedroom waiting for Sarah to say something to her when something clicked inside her and she realised that she was free. She could just go. She grabbed a bag from the wardrobe and threw in whatever clothes she could get her hands on and started to leave. Sarah sat there and watched, helpless as Tatyana's words paralysed her.

'Maybe Poppy will see what her mother is before it's too late for her.' Tatyana spat the words, hoping each one would land like a slap on her face.

Poppy's name snapped Sarah out of her trance of self pity. It took her a moment to realise what was happening. Tatyana was leaving. She got up from the bed, ran to the door and slammed it shut before Tatyana could reach the handle. She grabbed Tatyana's hair with her left hand and pulled it hard, yanking her head back. Tatyana stumbled off balance and Sarah slapped her viciously across the face with her right as she held on to her hair. She hit her so hard Tatyana fell on the ground.

'You ungrateful little bitch! How dare you talk about

my daughter like that!' Sarah stood over Tatyana who was now scrambling to get into a corner.

'I took you from that hellhole you called a home and stopped you getting farmed off to anyone and everyone.' The power in the room had changed hands, it was back with Sarah. She had no intention of letting it go again. 'I've given you a home, a bed, new clothes and warm food. This. This is how you repay me. By talking about my daughter like I'd ever let anything like this happen to her. You bitch. This isn't what I want. We all have to do things we don't want if we want a better life. I don't want any of this.' Tatyana had backed herself into the wall and curled up. Tears streamed down her face. She wasn't afraid of Sarah. She was scared she'd missed her moment.

Sarah sat on the floor beside Tatyana. Her anger quelled, her voice lower. 'I really don't want this but I'm trying. I'm sorry it has to be this way. It has to be better than what you were doing.'

Tatyana wiped the tears from her face and looked up. She saw the anger in Sarah, the desperation in her face and voice. She believed her. But this wasn't about Sarah, this was about Tatyana. She needed to be strong. This was her moment to break free. She needed to fight back.

'That doesn't make it right. It's not up to you to decide what I do. Or who I do.' She pushed Sarah aside, threw the bag on the bed and left the room. Her belongings didn't matter. They weren't hers anyway. She called out one final jibe from the corridor as she took her first steps to a new life.

'You'd better be careful or they'll take Poppy from you.'

Tatyana grew at least an inch as she walked to her freedom. She couldn't believe it. She'd travelled so far, endured so much. She'd escaped her brothers, she'd escaped her father. She was now leaving Sarah behind. At this moment she was stronger than she ever thought she could be. She held her head high, her new found confidence soared within her for three steps until she felt Sarah's hand grab the side of her head. She turned to defend herself but it was too late. Sarah slammed her head off the wall with such force that it knocked Tatyana out cold. Instantly her body collapsed in a pile on the carpet.

Coffee Shop

Remi decided to go for a walk after his chat with Sharon. His phone buzzed in his pocket, it was Louise. He didn't even need to check. She'd phoned him three times already. This whole mess was getting bigger than he'd thought. He needed to give his head some space to think, to pull at the threads and see where they led him. He'd return her call later.

Where did Giles slot in all of this? Was the relationship between Reinholdt and Marty Mason a sidetrack? Remi needed a strong coffee. There was a coffee shop about five minutes walk away. He decided get a table there and mull things over.

Then it hit him. A wave of nausea. Normally he'd phone Laura and check her plans before indulging in some time at a coffee shop. For the last few months their lives had been so intrinsically linked. Laura's pregnancy was difficult. Had been difficult. Remi had needed to be at her side throughout. Then there had been so much to do to get ready for the baby; the practical stuff. He enjoyed it but still wished for a little time to just himself now and then. Now that he had the spare time he'd longed for it felt hollow. Had his desire for space willed this to happen? He was almost sick at the thought. His emptiness swirled inside and left him feeling unbalanced as he walked. He pulled his coat closer around him and stuffed his hands deeper into his pockets hoping it would suffice to keep him from falling over in the street. A dust laden wind whipped across his face as he walked. A painful reminder that he wasn't dreaming and he wouldn't wake from his nightmare.

Lost in his own world with his head buried as far as possible into the collar of his black peacoat Remi didn't notice an old green Land Rover defender 90 pulling into an empty parking space and the driver get out and follow him.

Peter kept a clear distance between himself and Remi. Once Remi had gone into the Costa coffee Peter took a seat outside and kept a watchful eye from a park bench to make sure he was alone. It gave him time to finish the cigarette that hung from his lip.

He watched Remi order a coffee and sit at a corner table. After a couple of minutes Remi was still at the table on his own. Peter decided to go in himself.

Remi's attention was elsewhere, idly scrolling through his phone when Peter sat down at his table.

'I bought you a muffin.' Peter slid the plate across to Remi.

'Who are you?' Remi looked up from his phone and then around to see if there was anyone else about to join them.

'I'm Peter'

'Now's not a good time, Peter.' Remi returned his gaze to his phone. He was tired and drained with little patience for whoever this guy was. His casual demeanour masked his growing uneasiness at the presence of the stranger.

'I don't mean to intrude but I think you and I have something in common that I'd like to talk to you about. A proposition, if you will.'

'Not interested.' Remi shifted slightly in his seat.

'Tell you what. I'll leave the muffin, it's probably stale anyway.' Peter moved the muffin and side plate to the edge of the table while Remi watched him. 'I'll have my coffee in this seat, it's a nice view. Sometimes I like to talk while I have my coffee. If you hear anything you find interesting then I'm open to a conversation. My hunch is you might find what I have to say at least a little interesting, Remi'

Peter eased back in the chair directly opposite Remi and took a sip of his coffee. His eyes summing up Remi's reaction from over the top of cup.

'Un huh.' Remi disengaged from the conversation and returned his attention to his phone. Now was a good time to return Lou's call. He scrolled for her number and dialled. He held the phone up to his ear indicating wordlessly he was on a call. Hoping this was enough of a hint.

'As I said my name is Peter. I work for Giles and Sarah Marsden.'

This got Remi's attention. He sat more upright.

'Hello, Remi where the hell have you been?' Louise had picked up straight away and was on the other end of the phone. Remi didn't answer her, he stared at Peter as he sat across the table impassively. He had the look of military about him. Although older than Remi he was sure this guy could still handle himself in a fight. Remi's uneasiness grew even more. His experience told him military men who worked for wealthy civilians rarely took jobs that didn't involve intimidation. The scar that ran the length of Peter's cheek didn't do anything to dissuade this perception. Remi decided not to go on the offensive. Yet.

'Call you back Lou.' He hung up and put the phone on the table beside the discarded muffins.

'What brings you to my table Peter?'

'As I said I think we can help each other'

'I doubt it.' Remi sat back in his chair again, giving the appearance of physically losing interest in the conversation. Even though his heart raced and every sense in his body hung on Peter's words he remained impassive, 'I'm not sure why you're here Peter, but I'm a policeman. If you're here to give me some friendly advice then I suggest you leave. And quickly.' He took a sip of his own coffee to calm himself down.

'Not at all.' Peter smiled, hoping to reduce the tension he sensed in Remi. 'The opposite in fact. As I say I think we can help each other.' Peter leaned forward and held eye contact, he needed to gain Remi's trust. 'As I said, I work with Giles and Sarah Marsden. I've been employed with them for a number of months now and have been slowly gathering information on them.'

'What type of information?'

'Proof. I can show you where they are holding them'

'The goods? You've seen them?'

'Goods?' Peter was taken aback by children being referred to as goods. He decided not to make too much of a deal out of it. 'Eh, yeah. I've seen where they keep them. This last week I've been allowed closer access than before. I think I've now got enough evidence for you to arrest and more importantly successfully prosecute them.'

'Now you've got my attention. Tell me more.' Remi's phone started to buzz again. It was Louise. Remi turned the tones down but it vibrated on the table providing a background urgency to their conversation.

Peter became more cautious and looked around the coffee shop to make sure no-one was following him. He didn't like what he saw. There was a couple two tables away and the man kept looking in his direction. He wasn't sure if he was just being paranoid but decided to wrap the conversation up just in case.

'I can't go in to details here but Sarah is running a fundraiser tonight. If you can get yourself there then come and find me. I'll show you everything you need to make an arrest there and then.'

'I see how that helps me, but what's in it for you.'

Peter smiled. 'Let's just say I believe the world will be a much better place with people like the Marsden's not in it.'

Remi folded his arms his eyes searching for clues to Peter's motivation. After a prolonged silence he spoke. 'We can agree on that. Giles Marsden is a small time smuggler. Guys like him are ten a penny. But that's not why I'm after him. He took someone very special from me. For that he needs to pay.'

Now it was Peter's turn to size up Remi. He sipped his coffee without taking his eyes off the policeman he shared so much pain with. His mind started asking questions he couldn't answer. Should he tell him about Sam? Was he ready to? Could he trust him? Would he believe him? By the time he'd set his mug back on the table he'd decided.

'I'm sorry to hear about your wife. Believe me I am. I know the pain of losing someone close to you without being able to protect them. It consumes you. Many years ago I lost my only sister to someone. I've chased them ever since. The Marsden's weren't involved in her death but my search has brought me to their door. This is bigger than you think Remi.'

Both men recognised their own grief in each other. The trust Peter had wanted Remi now granted. Peter continued. 'The image we see of people is the one we want to see. It takes focus to see behind the charade we all live. You have to want to see what's kept in the dark. You now have the focus, that's why I've come to you. You don't know me and I don't know you. I'm asking you to give me some of your time tonight and I'll show you a world you never knew existed. What you do with it is up to you. Is that something you can sign up to?'

Remi agreed. 'I've been assigned to the fundraiser anyway. I'll see you in there and we'll take it from there. My focus is Giles Marsden.'

Peter stood up happy to have Remi onboard for the moment at least.

'Agreed. I'll give you him on a plate, and more. Giles sent me here to send you a warning to back off. He's an incompetent arsehole, but nonetheless I'd keep an eye over one shoulder. I don't know the full length of his reaches yet.'

With that Peter left and Remi remained in his chair mulling over what he'd just been told. Should he tell Louise? He began to eat the muffin Peter had bought him to help his thinking. His attention focussed on his muffin he didn't notice the man in the far corner of the coffee shop, just behind the couple that aroused Peter's suspicions earlier. He didn't notice the man had been watching his conversation with Peter. He didn't see the man reach into his pocket and make a phonecall to Marty Mason updating him with what he'd just seen.

MAMA

Poppy Marsden was sitting on her bed reading her latest favourite book; 'The Girl of Ink and Stars'. Her best friend in school, Sophie had lent it to her and she was absorbed in it. She loved to read, especially of faraway places and adventures. Anything to take her away from the house she lived in. A knock on the door pulled her back from the pages and into her room.

'Can I come in?' Sarah asked from the doorway.

'Is Dad with you?'

'No. It's just me. I wanted to have a chat with you.'

'I'm reading.' Poppy wasn't in the mood to have some girl time with her mum.

It was two days ago that she her computer had been taken from her. She didn't really care about losing the computer itself. She could use her phone for most of the things she wanted anyway. What she did care about was that it was always her who lost out when her mum and dad fought. Which was all the time. She wished they'd just get a divorce, it would be simpler all round. Most of her friends in school, their parents had split up. It seemed pretty cool. The parents would spend most of the time trying to get you to love them more than the other one so you pretty much got to do whatever you wanted.

Poppy didn't even like bringing her friends back home after school in case her parents were arguing. She felt more and more isolated as a result. Her other friends would all take it in turns playing at each others' houses but Poppy stopped getting invited and she could feel she was becoming more and more distant.

'You want me to brush your hair?' Sarah asked hoping to bridge the gap in their relationship. Poppy used to love to sit and let Sarah brush her hair when she was younger. At the time Sarah had thought those days were tough but now she looked back in envy at how simple they had been.

Poppy didn't answer but she turned slightly making more of her hair available to her mum. An olive branch. They both sat in silence as Sarah slowly brushed Poppy's long blonde hair. The gentle rocking of her head as her mum made long purposeful strokes brought Poppy back to when she was younger. When she was happy. Before the other children came to the house. When it was just her, mum and dad. She remembered the laughing and joking. She remembered one night they had been outside playing in the afternoon. It must have been winter because she had been cold. Mum and dad had brought her in for a bath and afterwards mum sat on the bed and brushed her hair like she was now and dad sat in the chair in the corner and read a story. Her smile was forlorn. Was she reaching for a memory she had only read about?

'Do you still love Dad?'

Sarah stopped brushing for a minute as she thought about the question. It was something she should have asked herself long ago but she had been too busy with everything else to even think about it. Poppy turned to face her waiting on a response.

'Yes.' eventually Sarah was able to answer. She was being honest, she did love Giles. 'It's just that it takes a bit longer to find it everyday these days.' The second part wasn't intended but Sarah was glad it came out. She hated lying to Poppy and even though she always thought she'd have been a better parent than she turned out to be she was proud of the fact that she didn't lie to Poppy. For the most part.

'What was it like when you first met dad?'

'How do you mean sweetie?'

'Well, you said it takes a bit longer these days. So it sounds like it wasn't always like that. Tell me what it was like then.'

'Maybe another time.'

'Ppppplllllleeeeaaaaassssseeeeee!'

Sarah smiled as she remembered back to when she and Giles first fell for each other. 'Your dad and I met one night outside the pub. Your father of course wouldn't have been seen in the pub but my friend had a flat tyre so your dad and his friend, Terry stopped to see if they could help. Terry later moved to Australia so you never met him but he would have loved you. Anyway. Terry did all the work while your dad naturally stood around and talked. They didn't really have anywhere to go that night so once the tyre was fixed your dad and Terry joined us on a night out. Well, we had the best time. Your dad couldn't believe the world we introduced him to. We went to a nightclub where we all danced all night. Then after the club shut I took your dad to a burger van and he experienced a gravy chip. For the first time in his life. He loved it. I loved it. And from there we had a whirlwind romance. I showed him a world he never knew existed. Filled with people who had a freedom he could only ever dream of. He took me to places I'd only ever read about. But it was more than the places he took me. It was how I felt when I was with him. People noticed me. They listened when I spoke. He made me... visible.' The memories were genuinely happy ones for Sarah and her mood lightened as she recalled them.

'Do you still love me?'

This time there was no hesitation. 'Of course. With all my heart. You are everything to me. And to your dad. We both love you very much. Don't you know that?'

'I guess so. It's just it doesn't feel like it sometimes.'

Sarah's heart broke. She looked directly at her daughter and cried. 'I know. I know things aren't great at the minute. And I'm sorry. I really am. But your dad & I...' Sarah searched for the right words. 'Your dad and I..., we are both trying our best to make things better. And even though we may not always do things in the same way or agree about what we should do, we are both trying. Really hard. Do you understand?'

'I suppose so.'

A knock came at the door. Sarah stopped her brush stroke half way down Poppy's hair,

'Hello?' Sarah rolled her eyes as she heard her mother's voice.

'Sarah, Poppy, I heard the shouting'. Margarite wheeled herself into her granddaughter's bedroom.

'Not now mum. I'm trying to talk to Poppy. Alone.'

'Well I *am* her grandmother Sarah. Perhaps I can help. Poppy darling, may I come in.'

'Sure gran, why not. Might as well have a fight in here as well.' Poppy moved off the bed and slumped into her chair that was constantly draped with clothes in the corner. Sarah gestured at her mother to leave them alone with no luck as Margarite wheeled herself into the centre of the bedroom apparently oblivious to anything her own daughter was trying to communicate.

'Poppy darling, I overheard some of what happened and I'd like to buy you a computer to replace the one your loser of a father got taken away.'

'MUM! GET OUT!' Sarah stood and shouted at her mother.

'He's not a loser, he's my dad!' Poppy stood up to defend her family. "For fuck sake" her words muttered in contempt at no-one in particular.

'Poppy! That's enough of that language!' Sarah now turned her ire on her daughter. Poppy knew better than to protest instead she slumped back in her chair and grabbed her phone. Sarah had completely lost any control of the conversation. She grabbed the back of her mother's wheelchair and started to pull her out of the room. Margarite feigned innocence in protest 'What? What did I say? I offer to buy a computer and this is what I get in return. Some mother you are, raising a spoilt brat like that!'

Poppy went to speak back but Sarah stopped her in her tracks with a look silently regaining control of the room.

She inhaled deeply giving her time to weigh up a response. Should she ignore the comment or defend herself as a mother afterall it's just one more in the thousand she'd already endured. By the time she had exhaled she chose neither.

It wasn't about her, this was about Poppy. Her little girl who had just told her that she felt unloved.

She let go of the wheelchair handles, purposefully walked around to face her mother. Poppy put her phone down to see what was going to happen next. This was more interesting than YouTube. Sarah knelt in front of her mother so she was at her eye level.

Her voice was calm but fuelled with venom as she spoke. 'My daughter. Your granddaughter is one of the most wonderful, loving, talented, funny girls I have ever had the pleasure of knowing. She is kind. She is smart. She is, quite frankly the best of all of us. She is the only remaining goodness in this house at times and the only source of pride I have in this fucked up life. You can keep your ill informed opinions to yourself. Get out. Go back to the room, that I and my loser husband give you out of the kindness of our hearts.'

Margarite slowly wheeled herself out of the room while Sarah and Poppy sat staring into their own worlds. After a few minutes Poppy broke her stunned silence with a laugh. 'I can't believe you swore mum! I'm telling dad!'

'Oh really? I think that would make your father's day to know I swore at mum!' Sarah laughed. It felt good to laugh with Poppy again. She'd pay for it later with her own mum but that didn't matter now. They both smiled, a couple of bricks had been removed from their internal walls.

'You want me to finish your hair?'

'Yeah'. Poppy sat back up on the bed and they both resumed their roles from earlier with Sarah brushing Poppy's long hair.

'Mum?'

'Yeah?'

'Thanks for sticking up for me.'

'Always'

'Did you mean what you said? About being proud of me?'

'Every word.' Sarah kissed the back of her daughter's hair. Poppy let her and they both savoured the moment.

'I'd better go and check on your loser dad and see what he's up to now. Are you ok?'

Poppy nodded and Sarah left the brush on the bed and went to leave the room.

'I love you Mama.' Sarah's heart skipped a beat. Suddenly dread pumped around her body. She froze at the edge of the bed. 'Where did you hear that?' she stared ahead, unable to look at her daughter.

'The girls call you it. I thought you liked it.'

Sarah closed her eyes to hold back the tears. She turned to Poppy and hugged her. She spoke with Poppy's head against her chest so she couldn't see the tears in her eyes.

'No sweetie, you're my daughter. Please call me Mum or Mummy. You're the only person in the world that can call me that.' Sarah left the room without looking at Poppy. She went to her own bedroom, shut the door, threw herself on to the bed and sobbed into her pillow. She had failed shielding Poppy from everything she was doing. Everything that she had to do.

Peter's fall

The late morning sun had just broken over the roof of the mansion's outbuildings providing scant warmth to a bitterly cold day. Giles's breath was visible as he slammed the shovel he was using into a pile of rubble and threw it into the wheelbarrow.

He was furious. His day had began with another argument with Sarah about money. It had started last night. Sarah had been upset about Poppy. He had tried to calm her but she refused to listen. Nothing he said helped. She kept telling him she'd failed her. She then brought up money. Again. When he woke this morning she was already up going through bills. Again it was all his fault. It felt that the only communication they had these days was shouting about money. At least this time Poppy had left for school and she hadn't been there to witness them fighting. Giles worried about what Poppy saw. His mum and dad hadn't had a great relationship. Their fighting was quieter though. It silently hung on the walls and in the corridors of the house Giles had lived his whole life in.

Sarah and him had passion though. These days there was more fighting than either of them wanted but they used to laugh. Lots. Now money was tighter the stress it created penetrated into everything. Like a heatwave, it was oppressive.

Giles felt he coped better. He knew they were in trouble but they would be ok. Sarah though, she had turned into a real bitch. How quickly she'd forgotten that he'd brought her and her bitch mother into his house. His family's house. They'd have nothing if it wasn't for him. He provided for his family. It's true some of his investments hadn't panned out as quickly as he'd wished but they would in the long run. You need to take some risks in life if you're to succeed.

He threw another shovel full of rubble scattered into the wheelbarrow. Manual labour wasn't his forte but it did have some uses in releasing anger. He dug the shovel back into the stones ready to load up again when his phone rang in his pocket providing him a well earned rest after ten minutes of hard work.

The voice on the other end of the line belonged to Marty Mason. His informant had relayed the details of Peter's meeting with Remi yesterday. Marty was not happy to be phoning someone he had little to no time for but it was the final phonecall that banished Theodore Reinholdt from his life so that gave him a little pleasure. He was curt as he spoke. Giles did not appreciate the information he was being told and only made noncommittal noises.

Marty Mason was the type of man that Giles saw himself socialising with. After Marty had finished summarising the information Giles tried to make small talk. He was dismissed instantly. This perceived slight only intensified his anger. He hung up and threw his phone across the walled yard. It smashed on the wall and the pieces fell on the ground. Giles was about to scream when he heard footsteps.

'Boss, you here?' Peter called as he walked around the corner, the ever present cigarette dangling from his lips. He quickly surveyed the broken phone and Giles' demeanour. 'Everything alright?' Giles let the handle of the shovel take his weight as he thought about what to say to Peter.

The phonecall that he'd just received hadn't told him an awful lot but it did tell him enough that Peter wasn't the unconditional support he'd hoped he would be.

Peter asked again, 'Boss? You ok?'.

'Yes, sorry Peter.' Giles waved him off. 'Sorry, you caught me day dreaming.' He feigned a smile and turned to continue with the stones.

Peter instantly knew something was up. Giles was as terrible an actor as he was a husband. 'You need a hand?' he offered with no intention of providing. He also knew Giles would see this as challenge to his manhood.

'No, no. Thank you. I need the exercise.' Giles shovelled stones slowly as he continued to speak. His mind was calculating. 'Tell me, how'd you get on with Remi, did you manage to see him?'

Peter was guarded with his response. Giles was zero threat to him personally but he didn't know who he was on the phone with that had warranted that reaction. He'd buy some time. After his conversation with Remi the noose was tightening for the Marsden's anyway.

'Yeah, I saw him'

'Well how'd it go? Did he take the hint and back off?' the noise of the shovel scraping the ground amplified Giles' annoyance at everything today.

'Not sure. I told him you were very sorry about what

had happened to his wife. But you'd been sentenced in a court of law and that was the end of the matter.' Peter finished his cigarette and threw it on the ground. He continued. 'I told him you'd appreciate it if he took the time to grieve his loss instead of chasing a non existent vendetta.'

'And he just accepted that, did he?'

'Can't tell. He doesn't seem to be the type to be easily scared. Plus he's lost everything. My experience tells me men like that are very dangerous.'

Giles stopped his shovelling and turned to Peter. 'You are telling me the truth, aren't you Peter?' Peter again played through scenarios in his head. Giles knew something, he just wasn't exactly sure though. He decided his best option was to play compliance. 'Course, why?'

Giles had him. He'd lied to him and he knew it. Now it was time to exert his power.

'It's interesting you say that. Before you arrived I received a phonecall from someone who saw you and Remi meet. Although they couldn't be absolutely sure about your conversation they were able to read some of it and they suggested that you came to some sort of working arrangement with Remi.' Giles leaned on the shovel eyeing Peter's reaction. He felt satisfied with himself.

Peter gave a half hearted laugh. Giles had shown his cards. He pulled another cigarette from his pocket to buy some time before he spoke. He'd underestimated the prick standing in front of him and now he needed to make sure he was able to finish the job.

He only needed one night. That was plenty of time to make sure Giles Marsden, Sarah Marsden and most importantly Theodore Reinholdt rotted in jail for the lives they've lived. For the lives they'd taken. He eyeballed Giles directly as he took a long drag on the fresh cigarette. 'Working arrangement? I'm not sure I understand.' The words formed around a cloud of smoke.

Giles came closer to him trying to posture his size in front of Peter. To intimidate him. It didn't work. His frame was similar to the shovel handle and Peter folded his arms across his chest and took another drag.

Giles had had enough of being belittled today. He certainly wasn't going to let this peasant in front of him challenge his authority. 'I'm not sure I understand either Peter. You see, you work for me. I pay you. You're nothing without me. I decide right here whether you have enough food to eat or not tonight.' Peter's eyebrows raised as he took another drag on his cigarette. Giles went in to assert his dominance. After the morning he'd had he needed to. 'You might walk about here with your combat trousers and the scar on your face and think you're a tough guy. You're not. I'm a tough guy. You didn't know I had people watching you, did you? No. Of course not. That's tough. Real toughness. You, you're nothing. Now get out of my sight.'

A smile stretched across Peter's face and he began to laugh. Time was up and he knew it. His time with Giles Marsden was over. This guy could enjoy his last few hours of freedom. Tonight night Peter would fulfil the promise he'd made to Samantha all those years ago. Giles and Sarah Marsden were the first piece in the puzzle. Theodore Reinholdt was next, but he'd fall easily. He could see it in Giles' eyes that he'd roll over on anyone he needed to save himself.

'Tough?' Peter snarled back and stepped forward into Giles so they were chest to chest. Giles stumbled as he tried to hold his footing. 'You're a pussy. The only people tough about this place are those girls you and your whore wife traffick through here. You're an embarrassment and nothing without mummy and daddy's money. Tough? You don't even have the balls to do anything to me yourself. You pay other people to creep in the shadows. You live off whispers. Playing games.' Peter flinched and Giles jumped a step back.

'Arsehole'. Peter's contempt for him was clear as he turned and began to walk away.

Fury rose up inside Giles and he shouted 'HOW DARE YOU!', Peter half turned to face him again. As he turned the sunlight flashed off the edge of the shovel coming straight for his head. Instinctively he pulled his arm up to block it but he was too late. The edge of the shovel caught him right across his temple and his body tumbled to the ground. Giles couldn't have aimed better if he'd tried. Peter was dead before his body hit the ground. He didn't even have time to think how he'd failed Samantha.

Giles stood over the body panting. His anger subsiding as the colour drained from his face. The rage that had come over him ebbed away as he watched blood trickle out from Peter's head and roll towards the stones he had been shovelling a few minutes ago.

'Shit'

Tatyana is getting ready

Tatyana sat on the edge of the bed as Anna urged her to keep still while she applied makeup to cover the bruise on her head. Tatyana's moment of defiance yesterday had earned her a night locked in the cellar that Sarah had rescued her from a couple of days previously. Her eyes searched the bedroom for answers. *Had Sarah rescued her at all? It felt like the same cell, was it? Did that mean Sarah had put her there in the first place? How can she escape?*

As her mind wandered Anna fussed around her dabbing here and there periodically taking a step back, admiring her work. 'No-one will ever know' she smiled as she finished.

'That's the problem.' Tatyana stood and went over to the mirror to see for herself. 'Here we are in the middle of this place in broad daylight. And no-one will ever know.' Her face was vacant of all emotion as she stared back at herself. She felt hollow.

Anna and Zusana came and stood beside her at the mirror. Anna spoke for the both of them.

'This is only for a short period of time. We pay our debts and Mama lets us go.'

Tatyana sneered, 'Is that what she told you? You

really believe that?'

'Yes'. Both of the girls nodded without a hint of doubt. This time Zusana spoke. 'There was a girl and a boy here before us, they left.' Tatyana turned from the mirror to face them directly. 'And two others before them' Anna confirmed.

Tatyana found it hard to make sense of what she was being told. She wasn't sure what to believe. She couldn't believe. But she had to admit there was something in the sincerity of the girls' belief that had her beginning to hope. Hope. It gives us strength we never knew we had. Tatyana wasn't sure she was strong enough to have it taken from her again. The faces of Anna and Zusana however belied a faith that where they were now was not an end destination, it was not a defined future. It was a point in time, something to move on from.

The floor was falling around Tatyana. She went over to the bed and sat down trying to steady herself. *Had she been too hard on Sarah?* Were the promises she had made been real, just delayed? *What if I have jeopardised my freedom? What have I done?* A nausea started to come over Tatyana as she sat on the bed. If what the girls were saying was true then surely she could cope for a while. She needed more answers, something tangible to hold on to, a number.

'How long were they here for?' she asked.

'I'm not sure but we only knew them for a couple of days before they said they were going. Then one morning they packed and left. We haven't seen them since.'

'Where did they go?'

'Don't know.'

'Did you ask Sarah where they went?'

'Yes, she said they had paid their debt and had now left to their own lives. With her blessing.'

Anna and Zusana looked at Tatyana, 'Didn't Mama explain to you?'

'I don't know. She did say it was expensive to live here and I had to do some things…' her voice trailed off as she was searching for a memory she was unsure she had. 'I suppose I didn't know it was for a short time' her voice now trying to pull together the thoughts in her head rather than talking.

'I don't know how long we'll be here for but I've been here for about three months, Zusana hasn't been here that long, just a month'.

'The men don't come all the time. Sometimes you have to sleep with a couple in the same day but that hasn't happened in a long time. Mama tries to space them out. We always get some time to ourselves. I'm studying to get my exams. Mama is helping me with that and gets me a tutor. Zusana is training to be a hair dresser. Mama was able to get her into the training school.'

'Exams, in what?' Tatyana was in disbelief. She couldn't understand what she was being told.

'Maths and English. I need them so I can study to become a lawyer. Mama says that's why I have to stay longer because she helps pay for my education. If I want I can stay with her until I get my degree or I can leave once I get my exams and be on my own. I'm not sure yet. I'll see what happens.' Anna shrugged her shoulders with the nonchalance of a teenager choosing what toppings they want on a pizza. Anna was flicking her hair and putting it in different styles as she spoke.

Zusana sat in the chair watching. She used her semi trained eye and gave tips from a distance.

'Mama says we need to be able to fend for ourselves before she'll let us go, that means having a job or being in education. She doesn't want us to, Zus, what is it she says?'

'Being trapped by a man. A woman's independence is her soul she says'

'That's it. She doesn't want us to be trapped by a man. Girls like us become dependent too quickly so she is helping us be independent.'

'Mama doesn't say independent though, she says free. She's helping us be free.'

'But our soul can't be free if we have debt. Freedom starts with financial freedom. Here we earn until we can be free. But we choose when we are free.'

A knock on the door interrupted the new rules of the game that Tatyana was only now learning.

'Girls, can I come in?' Sarah poked her head around the door.

'I hope I haven't interrupted.' The question hung in the air without answer. Tatyana tried unsuccessfully to make herself look busy while she sat on the bed. Anna and Zusana carried on with their hair display. 'Sure Mama, come in.' Zusana answered for the group.

'Thanks girls.' Sarah slowly comes into the room, the atmosphere making it clear she has interrupted an intimate conversation. Standing behind Anna she takes over the hair duties. Anna lets her and pulls a chair over to sit on as she does so.

Like fish when a shark goes past the conversation from earlier scatters and hides out of sight. Sarah has to nullify her threat for them to come out in the open again. She is worried her plans are unravelling in front of her and she has come to the girls' room to ensure Anna and Zusana are still hers. She also has to try and build some trust with Tatyana but that is secondary. This whole game only worked if the girls were indebted to her. If they understood that. Perhaps she'd chosen wrong with Tatyana. She had more fight in her than the others. The cellar hadn't broken her as it had the others. She'll need to make some changes to the process so that it works for any new stock.

She decides to keep things light, her words prodding at the unspoken dialogue in the room.

'How's your studies going Anna sweetheart?' Sarah specifically ignored Tatyana.

'Ok I guess. My tutor says I'm almost ready for the exams next month. I'm not sure. What do you think?'

Sarah stopped brushing her hair and looked at Anna directly in the mirror. 'I think, sorry, I know you'll do great. I believe you can do anything.' They smiled at each other and went back to hair dressing. 'And you Zus, how's your master plan coming? Have you found somewhere to set your own salon up yet?'

'No. Not yet. I spoke to an agent yesterday and gave him my details so he said he'd call if anything comes up. I gave the house number, I hope that's ok?'

'Perfectly fine. Now remember don't just sit around and wait. Did you tell him your budget? And don't forget we can get Peter to help out if it needs some repairs or anything like that to get it ready. You're not taking on a finished salon. Start small, don't bite off more than you can chew to begin with.' Zusana nodded in agreement. 'Thank you Mama'

Sarah stepped back from Anna's hair pleased with her

efforts. 'That'll work for tonight, keep it like that'. Anna twirled to get a look at it from all angles. Her smile showed she approved.

'Now girls, this isn't a social visit, I do have some news.' All three looked up at her. Sarah shoed Zusana and took her seat so she was sitting opposite Tatyana as she spoke. 'Tonight's fundraiser is going to be slightly different from what I had originally thought. There won't be the normal clients so I don't expect you to have to earn tonight'.

'Oh, but you promised tonight would be my last.' Anna interrupted. Visibly dejected.

'That's true. I did Anna, and I try and keep my word as much as possible. Now as I was saying I don't expect you to have to earn tonight but you may be called upon. That said Anna, the outstanding debt you hoped to clear tonight I was able to negotiate earlier with Judge Reinholdt and he has cleared your debt as a thank you. A personal thank you to you and as an apology to us all for an ugly incident that happened just prior.' Sarah held Tatyana's gaze as she made her point. Only once Tatyana looked away did she continue.

'What that means is you are debt free and have enough money to put a deposit on a small rental flat when you are ready. Personally, I recommend you stay here until you get your exams, moving would only be a distraction. But. That choice is up to you. If you stay and the opportunity arises for you to earn, then that choice is up to you. You may decline if you wish.' Sarah stood and gave Anna a long and genuine hug. 'I'm so proud of you.'

'Thanks Mama, for everything.' Anna returned the hug with mutual affection.

Sarah turned her attention to Zusana this time. 'My beautiful Zus. I'm sorry that tonight hasn't worked out as I'd intended. Hopefully I can carve an opportunity for you to earn. You'll be number one tonight. If it doesn't work tonight, then you have my word there'll be other opportunities, and soon. We'll get you to where Anna is. In the meantime keep looking for your salon and I promise you I'll be your first client.' Zusana nodded in acquiescence unable to look at Sarah. It hurt her that she couldn't earn, that she had to put her dreams on hold for another night, but the prospect of Anna leaving hurt her more.

'That leaves you Tatyana. Our new girl.' At the sound of her name Tatyana was pulled from her trance. Disbelief at what had just unfolded in front of her.

Sarah's tone was firmer as she spoke. 'Your debt is still full Tatyana. You could have made your first down payment with our friend the Judge but you chose not to and to embarrass me instead. The lovely Anna here has benefitted greatly from your actions. Do you understand?' Tatyana sat on the bed noncommittal. Sarah waited for a response but none came.

'I see'. Sarah smiled at Anna and Zusana. 'Girls I expect you to be dressed, ready and in the barn for 8pm sharp. Our guests will be arriving from then. I expect *all* of you to be ready.'

'Yes Mama'. Both Anna and Zusana replied. Again Tatyana declined a response. Sarah made her way to the door but stopped just before she reached the handle.

'Tatyana, darling. You'd be wise to speak to your friends here. I am a fair lady. But I expect to be treated fairly in return. I'll forgive our little...transgression earlier. Only once. Life here can be as tough or as simple as you make it. Either way, you will pay your debts'.

Tatyana's blood chilled. 'Is it true?' somehow her words found their way from her head and into the room.

'Is what true?' Sarah looked impassive hiding her disgust that someone would question her integrity.

'You'll allow us to go and be free when we've paid you back?'

'Of course.' Sarah was taken aback that she had to ask. 'You'll meet some of the other girls tonight who have already left, they are coming back to help'.

Tatyana was frozen in shock. She didn't know what to think. A moment of silence passed.

'Ok my dears, I'll leave you girls to have some fun. 8 o'clock, remember don't be late!' Sarah closed the door behind her before there was any argument. She needed to get herself ready and plan for the evening. She really was on the back foot now.

Inside the room Tatyana whispered 'Yes Mama'

At the fundraiser

Remi sat on his sofa in silence waiting for Louise and the team to pick him up for the Marsden fundraiser. The rented jacket was laid out beside him and his bowtie hung untied around his neck. Louise called his name as she knocked on the door. Remi involuntarily made a noise as he got up, in the same way his dad did around the time Remi began to notice that he had gotten old. The last few days had definitely aged Remi.

Louise was on her own when he opened the door, he stood in silence as he noticed how amazing she looked. Her long black formal dress hugged her figure and she wore her shoulder length hair down, it caressed the side of her cheeks. She looked so different from her normal team leader attire. It struck him how feminine she was. It was strange, obviously he knew she was female, but she was also his team leader. Standing at his door now though she was different. She was a woman. It hurt him. Deeply. As she stood on his porch waiting to come in he saw in her face a young girl with dreams, with fears navigating her way in life. In that moment he was reminded of everything that Laura lost, that they had lost together. He wouldn't get to walk his daughter down the aisle. He wouldn't get to grow old with

Laura. He wouldn't get to watch them get ready for a night out. He wouldn't get to buy Laura the wrong earrings. He would get to listen to her complain about the baby weight. He wouldn't get to see his daughter go on her first date, to go to college. To live a life.

'Come on in.' his words were distant as he moved away from the door to let Louise in. His mind was trying to hold memories that he would never have.

Although unsurprised by Remi's reaction she had expected at least some acknowledgement of how she looked. Tom had at least. His jaw dropped when she came down the stairs. She looked around the house, it was a mess. Dishes stacked in the sink. Clothes piled high. An outward expression of Remi's inward soul. She decided against saying anything. They both needed to get through tonight and if they fought now it would only be harder. Maybe catching Giles Marsden would help.

Remi grabbed his jacket from the sofa. 'Let's go!'

'You haven't even done your bowtie, come on Remi' he could hear the exasperation in her voice. It wasn't an attack, but it felt like one.

'I tried. I just can't get it tied. Laura used to do it. I didn't have time to buy a clip on' his voice trailed off as it begged her for help. His eyes were dry of tears but Louise could feel heavy sobs on her heart. Inside she cursed herself for being so thoughtless.

'Well I'm afraid you'll just have to make do with me. Take a seat' Remi sat his face level with hers looking dead ahead avoiding eye contact. Her hands worked swiftly betraying the amount of times she and Tom had to go to events like this through his job. When she finished she tilted her head to inspect her work.

Satisfied she'd done a good job she focussed her attention on him. 'You know Remi if you're not up to this…'

'I'll be fine.' He sounded as though he was convincing himself. Instinctively she reached her hand out and held his cheek. He closed his eyes and allowed himself to feel the warmth of human contact. He had missed it so much. He hadn't even realised he'd missed it until that moment.

'We'd better go before we're late.' It was Remi who broke the moment as her hand was penetrating the mask he wore every day at the minute and he wasn't sure how long he could hold it together for. 'Let me lock up and I'll meet you at the car'

Louise stood, straightened her dress and went to leave.

As she reached the door Remi called to her. 'Lou'

'Yeah' she turned, one hand on the handle.

'You look great by the way.' His smile was tender as he spoke.

'I know.' She playfully accepted the compliment. 'Now don't keep a girl waiting.' She closed the door behind her and let out a deep breath. She was already drained and the night hadn't even started yet.

When they arrived at the Marsden's estate Ben and Sam were waiting for them at the entrance of the fundraiser enjoying a smoke as the great and good of Irish life breezed past them and into the warmth of Marsden house. Both were dressed in black suit and tie. Standard male attire for any formal occasion. They would be wearing the same if it was a funeral, for a wedding they would at least change the colour of the tie.

'Don't you two scrub up well' Louise greeted them as she and Remi joined them.

'Not half as much as you ma'am' Ben responded as he stubbed his cigarette out with the sole of polished black slip ons.

'Careful now. Any more of that and I'll reprimand you.' She toyed. 'But thank you.'

'Any sign of Giles?' Remi's question reminded them they were here on business.

'None. But I assume he is inside. Looks like a champagne reception and cloakroom in the marquee and then people are moving in slowly to the old barn. My guess is he'll be there hosting with Mrs Marsden.'

'Well, no better time than now' Remi turned and began to walk to the marquee.

'Wait a sec Remi' Louise grabbed hold of his arm. 'I want a quick run through of the plan before we go in there.' She made sure she had the attention of all three before continuing.

'For absolute clarity we are here solely in an observation capacity. Everyone got that?' The team nodded in agreement. 'Good. Remi and I will stick together and stay in the function room. Ben, you and Sam split up and see what you can find, if anything.

'What exactly are we looking for boss?' Sam asked.

'Anything' Remi cut in.

Louise closed her eyes and took a deep breath. After a moment she spoke. 'I don't know exactly. But what I do know is this, I'm not happy about the way the last few days have panned out. Something doesn't feel right to me, and I guessing it doesn't sit right with you guys either. I've no idea what it is but there is sure as hell something going on here and I guarantee Giles

Marsden has something to do with it. Remi's right. We
need to nail this bastard for anything. But it won't be
tonight. OK? Tonight we go in, enjoy ourselves and see
what we can see. We make sure he sees us and we
leave. 11pm sharp. Observation only.'

'Got it' Ben and Sam agreed. 'See you in there.'

'Remi and I will follow you in a minute or two.'
Once Ben and Sam had moved out of earshot Louise
turned to Remi. 'Are you going to be ok in there?'

'Yeah of course' Remi was affronted she even needed
to ask.

'Just checking. I want you to be at my side all night
long, like a jealous husband, ok?'

Remi shifted his gaze to across the courtyard. 'Sure.'

'Sure what?'

'Sure, no problem. Jealous husband.'

'What's going on?'

'Nothing'. He kept flitting his eyes between her and
elsewhere as though he was sneaking a smoke at
lunchtime.

'Christ Remi. It might feel like it but I can assure you
we are not on a date. I am your superior officer. Tell
me what's going on, that's an order'

'I might have a lead'

'A lead?' Louise stood back in shock. Her voice
raised enough that some of the guests who were
queueing to get into the marquee stopped and looked
over at them both. Louise caught them in her
peripheral vision then directed her ire in their direction.
'WHAT?' she glared at them daring a response. The
guests quickly returned to their conversations only
stealing glances at the couple. Louise needed to have
this discussion elsewhere. She hooked her arm into

Remi's and pulled him to walk with her. She shouted in her loudest whisper. 'Chrissake Remi. When were you going to tell me about this so called lead?'

Remi stopped walking and stood motionless without responding. She walked in front of him and turned so she was facing him. This time she spoke softly. 'Remi, I love you. You know that.' She held his hands and she spoke. 'I cannot imagine what you're going through I really can't. But you need to be part of this team. You can't go rogue on me.' They stood in silence, Louise gripping his hand as she looked up at his face where he looked above her head. Eventually he looked down at her.

'I'm not going rogue Lou. I promise.'

'So talk to me. Please.'

'Look, it's a long story and to be honest I didn't say to you because I'm not sure if it's going to pan out, ok?' he could tell by her face that this wasn't good enough.

'Tell you what. If I find the guy I'll see if he'll meet you. If he's comfortable I'll signal for you to come over, ok?'

'Come over for what?'

'You can ask him what he knows. He told me that he'd give me the Marsden's on a plate tonight. That we'd have everything we need to arrest them, tonight.'

'Sounds too good to be true.'

'I know that's why I didn't say anything. Look, let me meet him, I'll have a quick chat and then I'll come and get you. OK?'

Reluctantly Louise agreed. 'Alright then. Now take me inside, it's freezing out here'

Hollow eyes

Inside the converted barn the conversation bubbled alongside the gentle tunes of a live band as guests mingled with friends and business colleagues they had or hadn't seen in a while. Women were effusive in their compliments of each other, the air punctuated with an occasional shriek while the men stuck to well scripted small talk. Business and golf. Arriving as couples and partners they effortlessly drifted to their natural tribes.

Remi and Louise hovered on the outskirts of pre-formed alliances as they moved between small groups balancing social politeness with wider observation. Ben and Sam had decided to ignore all social politeness and propped up the side of the bar at the far end of the room.

The band were playing Chuck Mangione's 'Feels so Good' in hushed tones as Sarah hitched her long green dress slightly so she could walk the three steps on to their stage. The music stopped as she stood infront of the microphone inviting her guests to grant her their attention as the evening was about to begin. Her easy smile masked the nausea and fear that swarmed inside her. Although well practised in hiding the constant gnawing at her stomach tonight it was rampant. She missed Peter. She hadn't realised how much she'd become reliant on him over the last few months. Just his presence had helped calm her. It was out of character for him not to show up. She couldn't shake the feeling that something had happened.

Her uneasiness had been compounded when Giles had suggested a peace offering earlier. As they were silently getting ready he brought out his mother's diamond necklace and asked if she would wear it tonight. Sarah had only ever seen it before. She had never been allowed to touch it. It sat in the safe along with some other high value items. Insured at just over one million pounds Giles had always said it was locked away to make sure Poppy didn't play with it. Sarah had always thought there was more to it though, as though he didn't think she was worthy of wearing it. She had suggested selling it once to help with their finances. Giles had become so angry and animated at the thought that she never raised the subject again.

She had nearly vomited when he put it round her neck. She had always known that she didn't belong in his world. As she stood in her mother in laws bedroom and looked in the antique mirror she saw the necklace around her own neck it only confirmed it.   Each diamond shone a light at her flaws, her insecurities and she finally saw who she was, who she had become. She had lost herself trying to hold on to something she never had. To live somewhere she never belonged. She begged Giles to put it back but he insisted. They'd had a rough time lately but they needed to turn the corner. Tonight was a new beginning. Although Sarah agreed, the sadness inside her weighed as heavy as the necklace. Tatyana had to be the last girl. The charade wasn't worth it.

She had sat on the edge of the bed in disbelief. How easily she had lost herself, her good intentions had been so easily sold. Everything she was trying to instil in Poppy she had compromised in herself. She had tried her best to hold her nausea but couldn't. As she was throwing up in the toilet Giles unhooked the necklace to keep it from getting splashed on.

The crowd were looking up at her expectantly but Sarah remained silent at the microphone. She had been standing there for at least and minute and it was only when Giles came on stage and held her hand did she realise that she wasn't speaking. His long forgotten touch pulled her back to the present.

'Goodness, I'm so sorry.' Her free hand instinctively went to the necklace and she regained her composure.

'You know I had a whole speech prepared filled with impressive rhetoric and statistics about the horrors of the world but when I stood up here I couldn't help but think as impressive as the speech was it wasn't as important as the people. Not just the young girls and boys that Better Routes supports, some of whom are here tonight. Tatyana, Zusana, Anna could you raise your hands please.' The three girls dressed in black trousers and white blouse were waiting staff tonight. All three dutifully raised their hands. Sarah continued. 'These girls are staying with Giles and I here until we are able to get them set up for themselves in accommodation and jobs so that they may lead very happy lives. That they may become independent. They are helping us tonight in order to gain new skills but also so that you may talk to them directly.' A number of men in the audience eyed the girls greedily as their wives were attentively listening to Sarah.

'Although the girls and boys that we help are so important and why we are here. I also think about you, our friends. Friends of Better Routes. About what brings you here tonight. With so many good causes out there all vying for your attention, and frankly, your wallets. I can't help but think it is because of who you are as people. Your goodness. Goodness doesn't know how much money you have, goodness doesn't care. Everyone here in this room is successful in life, that is obvious. But success is nothing without goodness and kindness, and this room has that in abundance. For that I am thankful.' The crowd gave a warm and polite round of applause. Over the years Sarah had become an expert in priming rich people to give. The next step was to add a little healthy competition in, but that would come after dinner.

'Before we sit for dinner I would like to say that it is my immense pleasure to tell you we have a guest speaker tonight, one of the very first girls Better Routes was fortunate enough to be able to help and who has done so well. She is thriving so we thought it would be great for you to hear directly from her about her experiences. She'll be joining us on video link all the way from New York. Thanks solely to your support. Now please I've rambled on long enough and our chefs have created a wonderful dinner for you to enjoy. So please if you could find your table, make sure you have plenty of wine and enjoy the dinner. After that we'll really party!'

Louise and Remi stood at the back of the room surveying everything around them. 'You know it does make you wonder how someone so good could end up with such an arsehole.' Louise pondered out loud as Sarah walked past Giles to mingle with her guests.

'Opposites attract, like you and me I suppose.' Remi's reply got him a sharp dig in the ribs.

'You see your guy?'

'No. Nothing yet. Either he's running late or he's not coming and it's back to just us.'

Each of the tables seated eight and were all round to encourage conversation. Remi and Louise had been seated further back from the stage. If they were at a wedding they would have been in the second cousin category. Sarah was playing the part of gracious host well and was stopping at each table to speak to her guests. Giles followed beside her clearly in a support role, polite and unobtrusive. Ben and Sam were sat at a table across the room with some older ladies who were clearly enjoying the attention and polite flirtatious conversation of younger gentlemen. From Louise's distance it appeared their marriages had lost their spark some time ago as their husbands were saving their charms for the waitresses when they passed in close proximity. The saddest part was they weren't even hiding it. Louise prayed her and Tom wouldn't ever get like that and made a mental note to make use of her brother to babysit the kids one weekend very soon.

Conversation at her table was much more stilted, driven primarily by Remi who wasn't great at the best of times but tonight he was restless. Clearly distracted looking for his contact and avoiding all interaction at the table. She leaned over and whispered in his ear. 'Why don't you excuse yourself, go to the toilet and see what you can find. I'll text Sam to join you and see if he's spotted anything. And when you come back I would really appreciate it if you were prepared to engage in conversation.' She politely took a sip of her white wine and turned to her neighbour. Mary, a lovely neurosurgeon who had recently retired and was ever so eager to preach to anyone about her new found love of open water swimming.

Remi didn't bother excusing himself. He stood up and walked to where he thought the toilets most likely would be. His focus on finding Peter while simultaneously keeping one eye on Giles had completely impaired his ability to understand the layout of the room and he ended up trying to walk to the catering exit. After he embarrassed himself again by walking into a busy kitchen he turned back into the dining room and finally looked around. Unable to see where he was supposed to go he gently asked a waitress.

'Er, excuse me Miss, could you tell me where the toilets are?'

The waitress pointed as she spoke 'To the left of the stage.'

'Thanks'

'You're welcome'. Tatyana forced a smile and returned to serving wine, her mind still racing about what was happening to her. Would she have to sleep with any of these men tonight? If she did when would she be free? Did she have any options at all?

Remi tapped Sam on the shoulder to follow him as he passed his table.

'You see anything?' Remi asked him in the toilets

Sam shook his head. 'Nothing. Only thing I can see

is there is plenty of money here. That's it.'

'Me either. I'm beginning to think the whole thing has been a waste of time.'

'Not a complete waste.' Sam finished his glass of what Remi assumed was vodka. 'Time for another.'

'Not too much. Something isn't right about the set up. I just don't know what. We need all our eyes on this.' Remi couldn't shake the feeling the waitress gave him when she smiled. There was something off about it. Like she didn't want to be there.

'You look perplexed?' Louise spoke through her wine glass and a polite smile as Remi sat back down. The main course, a choice between braised beef cheek or herb roasted chicken was being served and Remi took the chance to bring Louise up to speed about feeling something wasn't quite right. She listened intently with one ear, the other allowed her to indicate her comfort levels of vegetable and potato when it was her turn.

'Which girl was it?' After a minute of searching Remi saw Tatyana come back into the room with two bottles of wine. 'Her' his eyes pointing in her direction.

'She's one of the girls that Sarah introduced earlier, any wonder she's not that happy?' Louise challenged.

Remi countered. 'If I'd been rescued from sex trafficking and was living in a mansion like this place, I'd be a hell of a lot happier than she was.'

'Maybe. But don't forget these girls are carrying serious trauma. They're in a room of strangers that think they know them. Think they know your life. They're making judgements about you without knowing you. Look, see the pity smiles. Christ, I'd be miserable as well.'

'It was more than that though Lou. Her whole face

was hollow. Like she didn't have options, or control.'

'She's how old? 16, 17? At most. She's working serving wine to a bunch of posh arseholes'

'S'cuse me?' Louise's neighbour's interest piqued at the phrase.

'Oh not you Mary.' Louise quickly turned to her new best friend who she'd already agreed to meet up with next Tuesday for a quick dip and coffee. 'I mean creepy Simon over there.' Louise wagged her finger at the gentleman on the table next to them. His eyes had rested on every single pair of breasts in the room at one point or another. Mary nodded in agreement. Simon was creepy. His poor wife Tracy.

She turned back to Remi, 'Look. I think you might be looking for something that isn't there. But I trust you. So I'll make a deal. You enjoy dinner with me and our new friends. After that I'll go and speak to the girl myself. Low key. Not an interrogation, just some girl chat. Agreed?'

Old girls

Sarah tapped lightly on her wine glass to get everyone's attention. Chocolate mousse and baileys dessert had been served and guests had begun to move more freely around the tables and mingle with other people they knew hunting for fresh conversation. The generous levels of alcohol that had been served throughout the event so far were slowly grabbing hold of inhibitions and Sarah needed to hold their attention now or lose it completely for the night.

'Ladies and gentlemen...'. Her voice raised enough to be heard above the murmurs. '...if I could just borrow your attention for a moment.'

A hush slowly descended up the room as conversations stopped mid flow and guests returned to their seats. Sarah smiled as she gave everyone a moment to settle. Once they had, with all eyes on her she spoke again.

'I hope you all enjoyed what was truly a beautiful meal. I'm not sure if my dress will hold I ate that much. Can we give the catering team a round of applause to say thank you.' The applause was muted which shook Sarah. She had thought the food was delicious. It was to her, but to these people, most of whom she knew through Giles' or his family. They were used to much better.

'I do have a slight confession to make ladies and gentlemen, I told a little lie earlier. I said that we had a guest speaker who was one of our very first girls. That part is true. However we don't have one guest speaker we actually have three. It is my real pleasure to bring along two other girls, sorry, I mean women, who have successfully moved on from Better Routes.'

In the background one of the male waiters brought three chairs on to the stage. 'Joining me on the stage now I would like to introduce you to Anita accompanied by her husband Wilson as well as Tara. And joining us on screen all the way from New York we have the very first girl we ever supported, our very own Nichole.' All the guests received a warm ripple of applause as they arrived on stage to take their seats.

Anita and Wilson slowly walked on stage holding hands. Sarah greeted them each with a warm hug. Neither Anita or Wilson let each others' hand go as Sarah embraced them. The hug was reciprocated but the warmth was one sided. Giles was sitting at the closest table to the stage paying more attention to his phone than his wife so Remi allowed himself to watch with interest. Anita was small in stature and Sarah had to bend down slightly to hug her. Dark skinned with a natural prettiness Anita gave a restrained smile as she hugged her former mentor, or captor. Or both. Although restrained it was obvious to everyone Anita had the power to enrapture whoever she wanted with her smile alone should she choose to do so. Her clothes were in stark contrast. Plain and simple, bordering on drab. If pressed Remi would describe them as undercover clothes, in that they were chosen deliberately to make the person wearing them unmemorable. Both Anita and Wilson sat down quickly still holding hands.

Waiting just behind them was Tara. Taller than Sarah and more skinny than would be deemed healthy her black dress hung on her shoulders and nothing else. She smiled and gave Sarah a perfunctory hug back before taking her place next to Anita where she held her hand as well. They both exchanged a short whisper and faced the audience. To anyone who wasn't standing on the stage they appeared nervous, unaccustomed to attention. That wasn't the case. They shared a confliction. Neither lady wanted to be here. They had spoken together before they came on stage and neither understood why they'd agreed to be here. They wanted to be as far away from Sarah Marsden as possible. But they owed her everything. And in that sense they owed her as well. She had given them freedom and a life they could never have dreamed of if they hadn't met her. But they'd done unspeakable things to get that life. Unspeakable things that they wanted to forget about. To move on from. Being back at the estate flooded their senses with dreams that made them realise they couldn't forget what they'd done.

It took a minute for the large screen behind them to get a connection but when it did the beaming smiling face of Nichole eagerly popped up. Young and radiant, her face glowed with an energy Remi couldn't even remember. She instantly started to cry when she saw Sarah's face and started talking but the sound wouldn't come through. A short burst of feedback marked the arrival of Nichole's voice from New York mid sentence.

'- fantastic Sarah!'

'Well, I'll take that!' Sarah smiled. 'We had a bit of trouble getting sound through Nicki darling so we missed most of what you said.' Seeing Nicki's face on screen with Anita and Tara looking up at her was felt like a punch to the gut for Sarah. Their faces compounded her guilt about her decisions and how she had taken advantage of them to help her and her family. Nichole was the only one she hadn't. Nichole was how things were supposed to be. Before the debts came. A tear started to roll down her cheek.

'Nicki, if you don't mind I'll start with you just in case we lose connection again.'

'Sure'. Nicki's smile was so big it filled the whole room with joy to see.

Sarah half turned to her guests enjoying their tea and coffee as she spoke. 'Can you tell everyone here a little about you, about your experience with Better Routes and I suppose ultimately about where you are now and how you see your life now?'

'Oh my god, where to start. Well...' Nicki's excitement and enthusiasm overflowed from the screen. Her ams moved as quickly as she spoke as though trying to pierce the screen to touch Sarah. 'I guess I'll start with where I am now. So. I'm living in New York. I work in a fashion house as an assistant to one of the designers. I'll not name any names but it does rhyme with Prada!' There was a smattering of laughter from the audience. 'It's a tough job, I work really long hours but I love it and I wouldn't want to be anywhere else. And I wouldn't be here if it wasn't for the absolute saint that Sarah is.'

She became a little more subdued as she spoke of her

past. 'My dad used to abuse me sexually. At night after my mum had gone to bed he would get up and creep into my room. At first he only put his arm around me. After that he would guide my hand to his penis. After a few months of this he started to put it in my mouth and from there he progressed to raping me. I was twelve when I finally told my mum. She believed me thank god. She told me he raped her too.' Nichole wiped tears away as she told her story. 'She'd thought by having him raping her it would have kept him out of my room. It didn't. As soon as I told her she made a choice. Right there and then she decided we were leaving. She packed us a small bag each. My dad was a policeman and he came home from his shift early and found us.' Nichole took a breath and swallowed. Her audience hung on her silence. 'That night my mum stood up to him for the first time. She said we were leaving. Leaving him. He didn't like that. I suppose she found a strength she didn't know she had once she found out what he was doing to me. Mum fought back. He was much bigger and stronger than her.' Nichole was no longer talking to her audience she was back in the kitchen of her childhood home. Reliving the moment her life changed forever. 'Dad pushed her so hard fell over the table, knocking the clothes on the floor. He shouted at her. I think. I was screaming at him to stop. I grabbed his leg, it was all I could do. He kicked me away from him and hit the floor. I didn't see what happened next but I remember mum standing over him with the iron. She must have hit him. Dad was lying on the floor, regathering himself. Mum knew what was coming. She screamed at me to run. To get out of the house. To hide. So I did.'

Tears were now streaming down Nicki's face as well as many in the audience. Her story, infused with pride, anger, regret and hurt touched anyone that heard it. 'I kept running and never looked back. My mum died that night to protect me. He said it was an accident in self defence and had the iron mark to prove it. He was well liked on the force so he was believed. It was only when Sarah found me two weeks later homeless and starving that the truth came out. She gave me the courage to speak about what happened. He's in jail now and I didn't get to say goodbye to my mum.'

Nichole took a moment and held her eyes closed as she composed herself. She gave her face a wipe and then smiled back into the camera. 'But Sarah gave me the strength. She gave me support. She helped me through everything, ultimately becoming a second mum. Of course we'd fight, what mother and daughter don't. Please don't ask her about the time I stole her car to go and meet my friends.' The audience laughed almost out of relief. The horrors this young girl went through would be enough to fuel conversation with friends for a month but they weren't capable of staying in that moment too long. They needed brevity, before their night was ruined.

'But here I am. In New York living a life that I thought was impossible all those years ago...'. Nichole continued with Sarah asking the occasional question.

While the audience were engrossed in the stories on stage Louise took the opportunity to go and find Tatyana. She slipped away from the table noticed only by Remi who kept his eye on her as she found Tatyana standing at the back of the room holding a bottle of red wine and approached her.

'Excuse me, miss?' Louise tapped Tatyana on the shoulder.

'Yes?'

'My name is Louise, I work for the police. I was wondering if we could have a quick chat, if that's ok?'

Tatyana looked around to see if she was being watched. All eyes remained on the stage. 'Please.'

Suddenly shouts were heard coming from the bar. Sarah stopped talking and everyone turned to see what the commotion was. Louise's heart sank. 'Fuck.' She cursed under her breath. It was Sam. He was arguing with the barman. She half heartedly apologised with a raised hand and went over. Remi and Ben quickly followed.

'Sam. That's enough. Come with me.'

'But boss.' He was drunk but he still needed to make his case.

'But boss nothing. I'm ashamed of you. Get out. That's an order.'

Giles briefly looked up from his phone to see if he was needed. Seeing Remi heading over he decided to remain where he was. Sarah waited for them to leave the room before she apologises.

'I'm so sorry about that ladies and gentlemen. Hopefully he's left us something to drink!'

Her guests all smiled and returned their attention to the stage.

Only once the team had left did Giles get up to see what was going on.

Tatyana stood at the back of the room on her own holding the wine. *Should she follow Louise?* She had to, now was her chance. Her only chance. She put the wine down on a window sill and turned to follow

Louise out and talk to her. Sarah's back was turned and the door was just there. She walked with pace to the exit, to freedom. Every step she took she waited to be called. To be stopped. But none came. She walked past the bar, her eyes not daring to look anywhere but in front of her. She reached the exit doors. There was no one there. She began t quicken her pace. To get to Louise to tell her. To get help. She kept looking around her to make sure. Space opened up and she ran.

She ran straight into Giles who came round the corner carrying a box of wine.

'Tatyana darling, how good of you to help. Come, we'll top up some glasses.' Giles set the box down and got two bottles for Tatyana to hold.

Her heart sank as he opened them for her. As they walked back to the function room together he gently placed his hand on her lower back obliging her to stay beside him. She shuddered as he allowed his hand to fall and caress her bottom as they separated to play their different roles.

The decision

The team sat in an uncomfortable silence in Remi's personal Skoda Octavia as he drove them back from the Marsden's. Remi was pissed off. It had been a complete waste of a night and he drove fast and hard, the gearstick slammed into the next gear as the tyres screeched on the country roads. Louise sat in the passenger seat gripping the handle tighter than normal. It was a relief when Sam piped up from the back and said he needed a toilet stop. Remi swung the car into a lay-by at the side of the road and slammed on the brakes spraying gravel from his path.

After he'd finished his business Sam stood beside the car.

'Get in' Remi told him.

'Not until you hear me out. Hear what I have to say.' He'd tried to plead his case earlier but neither Louise nor Remi were in the mood to listen to him. As far as they were concerned his behaviour had ruined the night. Remi hadn't seen his contact. Giles hadn't one anything they could snag him for and Louise was concerned about what Bradley would say when he found out how the night had gone.

'Fine.' Remi put the car in gear and started to drive

off.

'Stop Remi.' Louise grabbed the steering wheel. He slammed the brakes hard. 'Christ Lou, what are you playing at?'

'What am I playing at? You're the one about to abandon a team member at the side of the road. Tonight wasn't great but we are absolutely not going to make it any worse.' She opened her door and half stepped out. 'Sam, get in. I'm tired, my feet kill me and I do not have the time for teenage dramatics. We can deal with this in the morning. We all need some rest. It's been a long week.'

Sam stood his ground. 'Not until you hear me out. I won't have you thinking I just got drunk.'

Louise rested her head face down on the roof of the car. Her salary definitely wasn't worth this. Fed up she stood upright then crouched down to look in the car at Remi. He continued to stare out the front window. Both of them were as bad as each other. Useless. She turned to see what Ben thought, hoping he'd have some sense.

'Hear him out boss.'

She opened the car door and got in calling to Sam as she did. 'Fine. Get in and we'll hear what you have to say.'

'Finally. Thank you.' Sam pulled the door shut and sat in the backseat. He leaned forward and rested one arm on the back of Remi's seat as he spoke. 'So as you know I do like a drink.'

'Clearly, short version please.' Remi vocalised his impatience from the front seat.

'I'm getting to it if you'd shut up and let me speak.'

Remi used the rear view mirror to stare down his

younger team mate. Scolded enough Sam carried on, this time leaning back in his own seat. 'After Remi and I had a chat in the toilets I went to get a drink. The bar had run out of Guinness, a crime in itself but I decided to move on to shorts. A little earlier than I normally would.'

'Get to the point Sam.' Louise put her hand on Remi's arm to give Sam the chance to speak. 'Go ahead Sam. Remi'll keep quiet from now.' Her eyes bore into his cheek.

'As I was saying. Normally I don't have shorts until much later in the night. However tonight that has helped us. I can hold my own with drink but by the time the vodka comes out it's normally at the stage of drink as quick as I can to get drunk. Tonight for obvious reasons that wasn't the case. Anyway. The first two or three were all fine. I took them with coke. But when I went to the fourth I ordered the same again. This time however it tasted very different. But as I say the coke masked a bit of the taste so I didn't think too much of it. Next time instead of asking a waiter I went to the bar and ordered a Smirnoff straight. Just ice. I watch as the Barman pours it from the Smirnoff bottle alright. But it wasn't Smirnoff. So I started to complain to the barman. That's when you came over.'

'That's it? That's the big apology?' Louise let out a long breath. 'Let me get this straight. You got into an argument with the barman at a function that we had to remain low key at. This argument meant myself and the rest of the team had to leave our surveillance duty. You then proceeded to have a temper tantrum like a toddler at the side of the road all because the barman didn't serve you Smirnoff? Have I got that right?

Christ give me strength.'

'Let me finish.'

'You had better.'

'The vodka he served me is exactly the same as the vodka we picked up the other day at Greenore.'

Remi turned in his seat to face him. 'What are you saying Sam?'

'I'm saying, if we're looking to nail this guy Giles for something I'm pretty sure he's serving the same booze that we caught being smuggled across the border. I'm not saying he's in on it but I do think that it's enough to look at him with a warrant.' He looked at Louise, hoping for confirmation.

'It's not Sam. We need much more than that. I appreciate what you saying but I can't see a judge granting us a warrant based on one taste test of a man who's already had a couple too many. No offence.' Louise turned to Remi. 'Let's go'

'Hold on hear me out.' Sam stretched out his arm emphasising his urgency. 'Ben, help me out.'

'Don't drag me into this.'

'When we are court the other day. Remi grabbed this arsehole by the throat. Remember?' They all nodded in agreement. 'Course'

'Well, do you remember who ran over and punched Remi? The same driver of the van we pulled over. Sarge, you and Remi had already left but after I saw Giles head over to him after. He referred to him as Mr Marsden. There's definitely a connection between the two. I'm telling you.' His eyes pleaded with Louise to believe him. After a moment of thinking her decision was made.

'O.K., look. If you're right then it's a good start for

us and maybe tonight hasn't been as big a waste as we all think.' Sam sat back in his seat justified. 'But, that's still not enough for a judge to give us a warrant.'

'Maybe not, but it's good enough for me.' Remi slammed the gearstick into first and spun the wheels in the gravel as he turned the car back to the fundraiser at the Marsden's.

Tatyana goes back

Tatyana sat alone on the sofa as she tried to get dressed. Her blouse hung unbuttoned from her shoulders. She couldn't face dressing fully and going back into the world. She just wanted to curl up in bed and cry. Outside the door Sarah was arguing with the man she had just slept with. His wife was still at the party downstairs so he was adamant about getting back before it was noticed how long he was away for. He wasn't happy though and he was making sure Sarah knew. Tatyana could just make out what he was saying muffled through the door.

'Sarah, I haven't got where I have in life by accepting just whatever people give me. That in there, that was like fucking a corpse. I expect better from your girls Sarah. In fact I pay for better. Now if you can't provide it then...' his complaint was interrupted by Sarah whose voice was much lower so Tatyana couldn't hear them. She did hear their footsteps leave. It was only then that she started to slowly get dressed properly.

Remi pulled the car into a pub carpark about a mile away from the Marsdens. The plan they had agreed on was to walk across the grounds and have a look at the outbuildings while everyone was still inside at the fundraiser. They should be able to get close and have a proper look without being noticed. Louise cursed their decision not to take a squad car, at least a squad car would have something she could have changed into in the boot. She decided to check the boot of Remi's car just in case. She was out of luck, it had one tyre iron, two old bags for life and a Tesco receipt.

'Right.' She closed the boot and turned to her team. 'We've already fucked this up once tonight. We're not going for the double. We're doing recon only. Enough to get a warrant. That's all. If we can't get it we leave it. Understood?' the team nodded. 'Let's go.' The three men crossed the road and hopped over a metal gate and into the field. Ahead was a small wood that circled the outside of the manor. That would give them enough cover. She hitched her dress and clambered over the gate as best she could as she mumbled something about chivalry. Her high heels instantly sunk into the mud as her feet landed on the ground.

Sarah stood taking a moment for herself before she went in to speak with Tatyana. She had finally appeased Robert Barraclough by offering him credit for another night. It wasn't that difficult, after all it's rather quite simple to get a man to agree to almost anything whenever you're walking towards his wife and he's just slept with an underage girl. She had no intention of honouring their deal however. She needed money and fast.

Tatyana knew Sarah's knock.

'Yes Mama?'

'Tatyana, are you ok?' Sarah sat down on the seat

beside her. 'What happened with Robert honey?'

Tatyana felt ashamed. She had let Sarah down again. She had tried. Tried to do what Sarah asked her, tried to work for her freedom. 'Nothing'

Sarah put her arm around Tatyana. 'Are you sure, you can tell me. Mama can help.'

They both sat in silence as Sarah noticed a tear escape from Tatyana's eye.

'Honey did Robert do anything to you? Did he hurt you?'

Tatyana suddenly looked directly at Sarah. Her eyes filled with anger. 'The man? Did the man hurt me? No. He just wanted sex. The man didn't hurt me. It was you. You hurt me.' Sarah calmly sat back in her chair. She understood why Tatyana was hurt. She'd been here before many times with other girls. But they do understand what she is doing. They eventually come around once they've paid their way and moved on. This was part of their cycle.

'I understand you're hurting'

Tatyana stood, her anger fuelling her strength. 'Understand? You understand nothing. You're worse than all the men.'

Sarah tried to give her a hug hoping that it would calm Tatyana. She put her arms around Tatyana who found her adrenaline draining from her, with it her strength went as well and she folded into the arms of mama. Her tears started to come quickly and turned into loud sobs. Sarah held her closely waiting for her to calm. Intentionally Sarah slowed her breathing down hoping Tatyana would mimic her. Tatyana's sobs began to ease. Sarah was slowly bringing the young girl in her arms back to her. Back to her trust. She whispered in her ear. 'Tomorrow we'll hang out and watch movies with the other girls. That'll be fun.'

'No.' Tatyana pushed her away. Confusion raced through her mind. She desperately wanted to be saved, to be free. But she didn't know who to trust. She went back to the last person she could trust and the words her grandmother used to say to her when she brushed her hair rang in her head. *'You can be anything you want to be.'* This is not what she wanted to be.

'No Sarah, it won't. I won't let you. I can't do this to me anymore. I'm worth more than this.'

Sarah tried to pull her close into her arms again. She needed Tatyana to trust her. More urgently though she needed to control the situation. She'd been away from her guests long enough and needed to get back. Tatyana pulled from her again.

'Tatyana, sweetie. I know this is hard. You're away from home, you're in a different country'

Tatyana snorted her face incredulous. 'You...You...I just can't deal with this' and she pushed Sarah as she tried to get past her and leave. Sarah grabbed her arm and pulled her back. Tatyana turned. 'I might be the one who is in a different country, but it is you who is lost.' Sarah froze. The words punctured all the reason and rhetoric that she had surrounded herself with and stung her heart in a way only the truth can. She lashed out at Tatyana slapping her hard across the face. Tatyana went to fight back but Sarah was too quick. She pushed the back of her head against the wall dazing her. Sarah didn't have time to talk this through with Tatyana and she couldn't risk leaving her here in case she ran away, or worse exposed her to the guests. She grabbed a handful of Tatyana's long brown hair and pulled, hard. It was enough to pull her off balance. She then marched Tatyana holding on to her hair through the back corridors of the mansion and straight back to the outbuildings where she'd kept her when she first arrived.

'Wait up for Godsake!' Louise wasn't used to bringing up the rear but her high heels and formal dress weren't exactly the best clothing for nighttime recon missions in the countryside. She was sure her dress had a new colour on the hem from being dragged across the fields and all she could smell was cowshit. Her left foot was already covered in it after she stepped in more than one cowpat. To make matters worse she could feel the manure rub on the inside straps of the shoes. It would take a weeks worth of scrubbing to get the smell off her. But at least the night was looking up, she was doing what she loved and they might be on to a lead.
'We're only having a look.' Remi shot back.
'Not a chance in hell I'm letting you lot go ahead without me. There'll be a perimeter wall ahead. Wait there and *do not*. I repeat *do not* do a thing until I get there.' She stopped and took off her shoes. Her feet were covered anyway and the heels had gone beyond inappropriate and were now actively hindering her from doing her job. She would carry on in her bare feet. It was pitch black and she pulled her phone out of her clutch purse to turn the light on hoping to guide her somewhat. Her battery was in the red. She'd just have to walk in the dark and hope.'

After she locked Tatyana back in the outbuildings Sarah went to her bedroom to clean up. Emotionally she was a mess. Tatyana's words combined with seeing Nicki on screen had more impact on her than she'd thought. She'd fallen so far from when she started the charity. And why? So that she could fit in to a life she was never welcome in? To hold on to a house that was never hers? To prove to Giles' family that she was worthy? To prove to herself she was? She'd have been happier living in a pokey apartment with Poppy and being free.

As she looked at her reflection in the mirror it taunted her. The family necklace she still wore looked like a Rolls Royce parked in a council estate. Lines that protruded from her eyes felt as though every lie she'd ever told herself was carved into her skin.

'No more' she said to reflection. She pulled three hairpins from her hair and her formal french roll came loose and fell around her shoulders. Her fingers washed away the Sarah of the past few months as they quickly styled her hair into a loose beach wave. She took off her dress and kicked it to the side of the room. Restricted no more she screamed as loudly as she could releasing her frustrations into the air. In the back of her walk in wardrobe she found her favourite dress. A light blue maxi with a boat neck. She hadn't been able to wear it in years. Giles didn't like it. Apparently it didn't suit the manor, or the people they were with now. According to Giles she had grown past that. She smiled, it wouldn't suit the party either. But it absolutely did suit her.

The last piece she needed to shed was her mother in laws necklace. It really didn't suit her new dress. She unclasped the back and threw it on the bed. Giles could put it away himself. It was replaced with a favoured boho pendant that hung off a leather string. She looked as though she was on holiday. She felt it. A holiday from the person she'd become.

A knock came at the door. Margarite rolled her wheelchair in. 'Your guests are looking for you dear.' Margarite stopped when she saw her daughter. A smile broke across her face. 'It's nice to have you back Sarah.'

'It's nice to be back mum.'

'I wish I had your strength sweetheart.'

Sarah lent over and hugged her mum for the first time in what felt like an eternity. After a moment Margarite spoke. 'I know you've got your party tonight but maybe tomorrow could we talk? I mean properly talk. I need to tell you some things, about your father. About Giles.'

Sarah stood up and sighed. 'I'd like that mum. We'll make some time together. I don't want to argue with you but Giles is my husband, so if you can't say anything nice about him I'd prefer if we didn't, ok?' she kissed her mum on the cheek and left.

'You alright boss?' Ben asked as he drew on his latest cigarette as he leaned up against the stone perimeter wall.

'I'm fine. Thank you Benjamin. Where's the other two?'

He nodded to his left where Remi and Sam were returning. 'A small cluster of trees just over the wall which will help with cover. Beyond that there are some lights which looks like a cluster of outbuildings. They're separate enough from the house that we could have a look there.' Remi spoke as he and Sam came into view.

'I told you not to do anything. To wait here.'

'We didn't. We went to look for you. About a hundred yards further down the wall has started to fall apart which gives us a small section to see from. It's easy to see.' Sam spoke trying to get back in the good books.

'Section of wall is so small you might be able to get over it, even in that dress.' Remi smirked while Ben and Sam tried to hold their laughs.

Louise couldn't help but smile. She was tired and pissed off but had to admit she was having fun. 'You lot are arseholes. And you definitely owe me more than one beer. Each. Now come on.'

They reached the edge of the tree line. Louise was about to give orders when the noise of a car engine interrupted the silence of the night. All four instinctively pulled back into the darkness of the wood to watch.

The courtyard is lit by movement sensor security lights so the team can see clearly as a small white van parks in the middle.

'Bit late for deliveries' Remi whispers to Louise.

She puts her finger to her lips giving him the universal signal to shut up.

As they watch the van driver and passenger get out and pull out two steel beer kegs from the back of the van and head into the outbuilding furthest from the house.

Both men return empty handed to the van.

'Storehouse?' Remi asks Sam.

'Looks like it. The kegs will be kept beside the pumps so that it's easy to change over. The bar had beer on tap but I didn't think they'd have their own keg room. How the other half live.'

The passenger pulls out a wooden crate holding four large spirit bottles and heads back over to the building. The driver closes the van door and pulls out a cigarette. He turns facing the team as he lights up. The underdeveloped moustache hasn't grown since they pulled him over just outside Greenore.

The raid

The sun was barely sneaking through the branches of the trees that line the pub carpark the team used last night. Remi is standing away from the main group of officers who are chatting and checking their equipment beside Ben and Sam.

'You think we'll nail him Remi?' Sam breaks the silence, breath mixed with steam from his takeaway coffee

'Hope so. We'll see.'

Louise comes over, more suitably dressed this morning in her standard issue fatigues.

'No heels this morning boss?'

'I've had three hours sleep. I can't drink my coffee because I can still smell the shit hanging off me from last night. Read the room Ben.'

'Sorry ma'am.'

'The warrant has come through. We're lead team. I'm knocking the door. Sam, Ben you're with me. Remi, I want you in the background away from any members of the family. The warrant is for the outbuildings only, which is fine. We know where we are looking. In and out. If we do our jobs right this bastard will be in the station by breakfast. Everyone agreed?'

Sarah sat alone at the kitchen table in her dressing gown. Giles and Poppy were both still in bed. A fresh coffee in her hand she peered at her computer screen as she went through the monthly expenses of the manor. She hadn't slept. No matter how hard she tried she couldn't get her mind to quiet enough to let her. Last night was the last time she was ever going to use the girls again.

She needed to find savings otherwise they would lose the manor. Although how she felt this morning she'd give it away.

Stupidly she'd tried to talk to Giles last night but he'd got drunk and they'd argued. Again. She suggested they needed to consider selling some assets, but he flew off the handle. He had said she was ungrateful wouldn't be anything with him. Without his family. Her heart was punctured again. He'd confirmed everything she thought. She was beneath him, beneath them.

The clock on the wall chimed announcing it was half seven. Poppy had swimming so Sarah needed to wake her soon otherwise she'd be late. There still wasn't any sign of Peter, his absence only pronounced Sarah's feeling of loneliness. Something was wrong, he wasn't the type to just leave without giving notice.

The heavy knock on the door pulled her away from her spreadsheet. Sarah hoped it was Peter, that he'd just forgotten his key. She opened the front door and saw Louise standing there with what looked like a football team of police officers. Sarah didn't think her heart could sink further but it did.

'Sarah Marsden?'

'Yes. What's wrong?'

'Sarah Marsden, we have reason to believe you are holding illegal alcohol and cigarettes on your premises and are involved in a smuggling operation. We have a warrant to search the outbuildings of your property and seize anything we feel is relevant to this activity. Do you understand?' Louise was impassive as she explained what was going on. She could see in Sarah's eyes she was confused. And terrified.

'I'm sorry, pardon, what?' Sarah can't grasp what was happening.

'Mum?' she turned round. Poppy was standing in the stairs rubbing her eyes. 'What's going on?'

'I'm not sure honey. Come on and let's get you some breakfast before swimming.' Sarah cuddled her daughter then turned to Louise. 'If it's for the outbuildings, you're not coming in the house. Go round the side. I'll be out in a minute.' She shut the door.

Her mind raced as she poured Poppy her shreddies.

'Is daddy in trouble again mummy?' Poppy asked.

'I'm not sure sweetheart. Mummy's not sure'.

Smuggled alcohol had Giles written all over it. He really was becoming more trouble than he was worth. She'll have to deal with whatever comes from that later. Her immediate problem was Tatyana. She was still holding Tatyana in the cell outside. The cell backed on to the keg store. Her only saving grace was it was only accessible through a false wall from the other side. She'd made it as invisible as possible but if the police were searching in there they would find it. It was invisible enough to miss on a daily basis but it wouldn't withstand the scrutiny of a police search.

Sarah left Poppy to her cereal and quickly threw a coat over her dressing gown to head outside and see if she could head the police off. She was too late. The courtyard looked like a movie set as it swarmed with police all dressed in their blues. The bulk of the contents from each of the three outbuildings were lying in the courtyard. Sarah could see a crate. It held what looked like vodka in the middle of the yard. She had been with Poppy no longer than five minutes. They clearly knew what they were looking for. Her head spun. She stood motionless as she watched policemen come in and out of the keg store. Her worst nightmares were starting to come true.

Muffled noises outside her cell waken Tatyana. Now she is alert, afraid. These are new noises. There's more of them and they are loud. What's happening? Is Sarah coming for her? Fear grips her cold body. Has she pushed Sarah too far? She scurries back into the room away from the sealed door. Her back hits something. She freezes. This is new. It wasn't here before. She sits motionless, unsure why. She waits for something. Anything to happen. Nothing does. Slowly she puts her hand behind her to feel it. The fingers of her left hand touch it. She pulls her hand back not knowing why. It's cold. And damp. Again nothing happens.

She reaches behind for a second time. She is slightly braver. Her hand is more open and she lets her fingers rest on it. It has bristles that poke her. There is something comforting about the bristles. Then she remembers the feeling. It feels like a carpet that has been rolled up. Tatyana laughs and leans up against it.

She's in a store room. Her fears subside a little.

Sarah stood close to Louise trying to make conversation with Louise. She is struggling to get her attention, Louise's only focus at the minute is her work which is hard enough. She hasn't been this sleep deprived since her youngest was in nappies. She needed to make sure the search was done by the letter. There is no way in hell she was going to give this prick any opportunity to get off the hook this time. She also needed to keep a close eye on Remi, making sure he is in check. She watched him intently as he prowled around the courtyard like a caged lion waiting for someone to throw him a steak.

Louise cut Sarah short, 'Is your husband around Mrs Marsden?'

'I think he's sleeping, why?'

'I presume there's no paperwork for the alcohol we've found so you'll both have to come down to the station until we can figure out where it came from.'

'WHAT THE FUCK IS GOING ON?' Every officer in the courtyard stopped at turned. Giles appeared at an upstairs window and screamed his disapproval at what he saw.

Louise looked at Sarah. 'I think he's up now.'

'Christ'. Sarah turned on her heels to head him off before he made things much much worse. Before she could get to him an officer came out of the keg room and shouted for Louise. 'Ma'am! In here.'

Sarah's heart stopped. She froze for an instant then decided to follow Louise. Inside the keg room the officer was standing beside two kegs of beer. Louise assumed they were the ones delivered last night as they were the only ones not connected to pipes. 'Bring these two…' Louise's orders were cut short by a loud commotion and officers shouting commands outside in the courtyard. All three ran out to see what was happening.

Giles stood in the courtyard wearing just pyjama bottoms and brandishing a shotgun demanding to talk to whoever is in charge. Louise spoke in Sarah's ear as she pulled her by the elbow. 'You come with me, maybe you'll be able to talk some sense into him.' To her right Louise saw Remi walking closer and closer to Giles. She needed to intervene before they lost control of the whole situation. 'Remi, stand down. That's an order. All of you stand down.'

Remi stopped walking but held his gun facing Giles. Every officer mirrored Remi, their weapons all trained on Giles Marsden.

'Mr Marsden, I am Detective Sergeant Louise Massey. I'm in charge of this search. Here's our warrant.' She handed him the paper.

'Let me see that!' he snatched it out of her hands and in doing so dropped the shotgun. Louise kicked it to the side.

'Ben. Take that gun away from Mr Marsden before he does some damage he can't get out of.' Ben quickly grabbed the shotgun from the floor and disarmed it, two shotgun shells bounced on the concrete as he did.

After reading the warrant Giles realised the trouble he was in and needed to regain the upper hand proclaimed loudly. 'This is an outrage. I'll be making sure my lawyer hears of this.'

'As is your right Mr Marsden.' Louise breathed a sigh of relief, crisis averted for now. 'May I suggest

you and your wife grab a cuppa in the kitchen. I'll call
you when we're finished.'

Disappointment

Sarah and Giles sat in silence at the kitchen table with Poppy who had refused to go swimming and frankly neither of them had had the energy to fight her. They had been joined by the family lawyer Richard Young from Mason and Jones law practice. Sarah had brought him up to speed concerning the morning events over coffee while Giles had decided to take a shower hoping to wash his hangover away. Richard was on the phone to the office when Giles came back looking fresher and calmer than he had been twenty minutes ago.

Richard swiftly brought the conversation to an end and hung up.

'Giles, have a seat. Please. I've had a look through the warrant. Of course it's above board and legitimate. But we need to have a serious conversation. All of us together. Sarah, would it be prudent if Poppy could watch some cartoons next door while we chat?'

'Yes. Of course. Come on Poppy sweetie. Give mummy and daddy a minute to chat. I'll be in as soon as I can.'

Richard continued once Sarah returned. 'As I was saying. The warrant is all above board. However it is very specific. This raises questions. They knew exactly what they were looking for and where it most likely would be. Do either of you know why that is?'

'Aren't you going to ask us if the booze is stolen?'

Richard smiled. 'No Sarah I'm not. It's as clear as day the booze is not stolen. They know that. What it is however is allegedly smuggled and potentially counterfeit. The counterfeit charge is difficult to prove unless they caught you selling it. That leaves smuggling which is most likely what they will aim to convict on. I am assuming neither of you brewed this yourself or smuggled it yourself?'

For once both Giles and Sarah were in agreement. Neither of them had done either.

'Good. I thought so. Any chance of a top up?' Richard nodded at Sarah who he clearly viewed as there to help serve. 'I'm afraid one of my many faults is I drink far too much coffee especially at this time of the morning.'

Sarah had never liked Richard. She had married into the family money and he knew it. She hated the way that he smarmed over Giles whenever they spoke. Some would say he was old fashioned and spoke to the man of the house. Sarah knew better. Richard Young naively thought Giles was the one with the money. It was the prospect of being around it that lured him in. She laughed at the way he sidled up to Giles hoping to get more money. They had inherited the services of the law firm from his father and had another fourteen months to go on the retainer before it ran out. Just like everything else. She couldn't tell you why but she really didn't like him this morning. Probably because she didn't like anyone this morning. She watched him as the kettle boiled. He was becoming more comfortable in her home than she would have liked. When he talked he absentmindedly preened himself. Ironing out creases in his suit that weren't there with his hands. Fixing his trousers every time he crossed his legs. She assumed it was so he could make sure everyone knew how much money he had without actually showing his bank account. He had never used any of her girls but she had no doubt he would if she'd offered. Everything about him was grotesque. She had used men like Richard Young to help her family, to help Poppy, to help Giles. She knew it was grotesque. That part of her. Watching him preen at her kitchen reminded her just how awful she had become. She plonked his coffee in front of him making sure it splashed on his blue suit. 'You might not be that concerned Dickie, but we are.'

Richard smiled as he wiped his trouser leg with a silk handkerchief he kept with him at all times. He hated being called Dickie but these two were prime clients and he had to take insults like that on the chin. Their retainer paid for the Maserati parked out front as well as an ex-wife and it was due for renewal next year. He needed to keep them as clients.

'I understand this is a concerning time Sarah and I apologise if I'm coming across cavalier. I don't mean to. I mean to say that in the eyes of the law there is a significant difference between the allegations. And we must be mindful of both. Now, where did you get the alcohol?'

Sarah ignored the question and looked at Giles to answer. After a moment of silence he spoke up. 'I bought it'

'Do you have a receipt?'

'I paid cash'

'Do you know the people you bought it from?'

'Not really. I met them in the pub and got talking. I was complaining about the price of a drink. One thing led to another and I'd bought a couple of kegs and some spirits to help with Sarah's fundraiser.'

'Don't bring my fundraiser into this. I didn't ask you to do anything of the sort. I had donations from reputable companies. This is nothing to do with me or the charity Giles.'

'Of course not.' exasperated Giles rubbed his head with his hands. 'Of course not. It's just we've been fighting so much lately that I thought it would be a nice thing for you. If I could help out with something that was so important to you. That's all.' His eyes pleaded for mercy from his wife. She reached out and held his hand, granting it. Hoping to find a way past this and move on as a family.'

'Mummy, can I have some water?' Poppy stood at the door afraid to come in to the adult conversation.

'Of course sweetie. I'll get you some.'

'Come here and sit on dad's knee.' Giles held his arm out in a show of fatherly affection that Sarah assumed was for Dickie's benefit. She hated herself for holding his hand so readily.

'That leaves us with the other question. Is there any reason why they would know exactly when and where to look? My experience tells me police are never that lucky without some form of inside knowledge.'

'Inside knowledge? Are you suggesting that I phoned the police about booze that I didn't even know about?' Sarah was outraged. 'Or Giles for that matter sent them a tweet and told them about his own plan? Fuck sake

Dickie get a grip. Sorry Poppy. Close your ears. Mummy is just upset.'

Richard was about to retort when Giles spoke up. 'We haven't seen Peter in a couple of days.'

'Peter?' Richard asked.

'No. No way. Peter was like family.' Sarah couldn't believe it. She wouldn't believe it. She had trusted Peter. In a way she'd loved him. He was everything Giles wasn't. He was like a brother to her. She'd even let him help with Tatyana. He knew what she was doing. He hadn't said anything. If Peter had said something to the police then she really was in trouble. It did fit, they hadn't heard from him in days. She gagged at the prospect. Was the raid a cover just to see what else they could find? The very thought of it made her sick to her core. She could feel the colour draining from her face.

'Sarah, I think the world of Peter as much as you, but it fits. We haven't seen him in a couple of days and then the police show up.'

Sarah looked at her husband as he held her daughter. Her mind was on fire. She needed some air. Just then a knock came at the internal kitchen door and they all turned. Louise was standing in the doorway of the kitchen with Remi behind her in the hall.

'Sorry for interrupting. Just to let you know we've finished the search. We've found…'

'Richard Young, the Marsden's lawyer.' Richard stood up as quickly as Louise raised her eyebrows at his interruption. Oblivious he continued. 'My clients have already told me what has happened and it is a very unfortunate mistake. If…'

'Mr Young did you say?' Louise wasn't in the mood.

'Mr Young. You can advise your clients that they'll need to come and make a statement in the station within 24 hours. We have also confiscated the contraband.' Louise turned and left.

Richard saw this as an invitation to continue the conversation elsewhere and ran after her immediately with Giles and Sarah in tow just behind.

'Excuse me.' Richard was keen to show his worth and impress his services upon Giles. 'I'm afraid I didn't get your name officer?' Louise stopped at the front door. Remi remained silent by her side. He recognised Richard from when his visit to Mason and Jones but didn't say anything. Louise could feel Remi tense, hoping for a fight. He needed one. He needed to unleash his anger. She feared it coming at the wrong time. Like now. She exhaled before answering.

'Detective Sergeant Louise Massey. Massey is spelt with two 'S's' for reference. Her smile could cut glass.

'As I was saying Detective, my clients-'

'And as *I* was saying Mr Young. Your clients will be required to make a statement at the station within 24 hours where an officer will happily sit and listen to everything they and you have to say.'

Never one to back away from verbal sparring session Richard was primed to interject when Louise continued. 'Mr Young. I appreciate you are defending your clients. I am sure they appreciate it too. However it isn't even ten o'clock and we have already taken up an awful lot of your clients' time.'

Doing her utmost to remain calm she spoke calmly with authority. The situation felt like it could deteriorate any moment. She could feel Remi itch as he stood beside her. She needed to get herself and Remi out of the house as quickly as possible.

Giles seeing a moment to assert himself as someone not to be trifled with moved infront of Richard. Still holding Poppy in his arms he shifted her weight to his left side ensuring she was between himself and Remi. 'Detective, I assure you this is all one big misunderstanding. I can also personally guarantee I'll make myself available to give a statement as soon as is convenient to us.'

'Thank you Mr Marsden. I think we have inconvenienced you enough for this morning.' Louise opened the door relieved to be leaving. But Giles couldn't let them go. He needed the last word.

'You're right detective, it has been a long morning. We're all a little tired.' Louise braced herself as Giles continued. She knew that he was about to do something stupid.

Giles looked directly at Remi as he spoke. 'I think we all need to go home and spend a little time with our families.'

A new lead

The inside of the bar room was quiet. Dylan the barman was getting on with his daily duties of mopping the floor and washing glasses as Remi propped up the end of the bar nursing his pint of lager. Louise had given him the day off and he hadn't felt like going home to an empty house. He might as well sit in an empty bar. Not that being there was helping either. After Giles' remark he had lunged at him. Giles being the coward that he was stepped back and put his daughter between them both. Remi had barely stopped himself before he made contact with Poppy.

After that it was pandemonium. Poppy was screaming. Sarah had tried to grab her. Louise jumped in the middle between him and Giles knocking Giles into a window in the process. The overly groomed lawyer shouting about suing. It took at least ten minutes to get Louise and Remi out of the house. Remi was pretty sure he'd be facing another official complaint when he went back to the office. Louise was already there, most likely getting her head chewed off by Bradley.

He took a swig of his pint as he mulled over the mornings events. He felt for the girl. Not because of what he had done. Because she had a dad who used her to protect himself. He would have laid down his life to protect his little girl from an harm. Now he would never get the chance to show her how much he loved her. He drank the rest of his pint alone. Grief his only companion.

With no reason not to order another one Remi waved his empty glass in Dylan's direction. The barman grabbed a clean glass and pulled Remi a fresh pint. The taps splurted as he poured.

'All ok?' Remi asked

'Yeah. It's just the end of the keg. Gimme a sec, I have to nip next door and change it. Back in a min.' In less than a minute the barman was back and running a dump pint through the taps before pouring Remi his second of the morning.

'You changed that pretty quick.' Remi was making small talk.

'Yeah, I've done it once or twice.'

'I s'pose. Did you run to the keg store?'

'Huh?' The barman was puzzled.

'The keg store. It's outside, you must be quick to get there and back in that time.'

'Not really. Kegs are kept close by. Makes it real easy.' Dylan smiled and set the now settled fresh pint in front of Remi.

'Cheers.'

Tatyana sat huddled in the cell. Cold and tired. But this time she knew she wasn't in danger. The real danger was outside. The cell had become her comfort. The distant voices she'd heard had gone leaving her with just her thoughts and her memories. A mind is a double edged sword. It can be the most powerful tool or most destructive weapon anyone possesses. It all depends on how you use it. Now she doubted if she'd made the right decision not to scream out. Her mind was playing tricks on her. Had she dreamt she'd heard the voices? How long would she be in here this time?

Tatyana knew she needed to control her thoughts. She needed a plan to get out, not just from the cell, but from the grasp of Sarah Marsden. Sarah had been very clear what was expected of her. The isolation of the cell had given Tatyana the clarity she needed. She wouldn't bend to Sarah's will.

Every plan starts with one movement. Tatyana's started now. She closed her eyes and started to feel her way around the cell again. Her hands slowly moved across the stone floor, along the exposed brick walls. She began to re-familiarise herself with her cage. Nothing had changed. The air was heavier than she remembered and it smelt worse but was still as secure as it was before. The only thing that had changed was the carpet that lay rolled up at the far end. The carpet. It was something. She could at least it might make her stay a little less horrible. If it was dry on one side she could sit on it. She could rest on it.

The bar door banged open as one of the regulars walked in dripping in rain. Cursing he took off his coat and threw it on the back of the chair.

'Guinness Bob?'

'Aye Dylan, please.' Bob didn't make eye contact with the barman as he spoke. He was too busy wrestling the scarf around his neck. 'Great day for ducks!' he proclaimed to no-one and everyone at the same time as he finally removed the wool burden from his neck and plonked his suitable large frame on a seat at the bar. 'You gonna put the fire on Dylan? Dry these clothes of mine out?' Bob had the ease of someone who was settling in for a long day of indoor recreation.

'Sure. I'll get it going in a minute.'

Remi sat staring into his pint hoping to avoid any conversation that was going to come his way. He really wasn't in the mood. Unfortunately he'd changed out of his police fatigues and was in casual jeans and a jumper. Police apparel was a perfect barrier between him and unwanted conversation.

'No coat today lad?' Bob was much happier to indulge in the small talk of strangers. Remi smiled and shook his head. 'Not today mate.'

Dylan poured the Guinness and again the pump began to splurt as he did so. 'Typical. Gotta change the keg Bob.'

'Sure. Take your time.' Bob was unfolding his racing post with little interest in what Dylan was doing.

Once he returned Dylan went through the ritual of running the taps before serving a customer. Remi watched with interest. 'Twice in one morning, that unusual?' he called to Dylan.

'Eh, not really. Depends on the customer base really. Here we have a pretty even split of Guinness and lager drinkers so if you're changing one keg you can be sure you'll change another one soon enough after. I've worked nightclubs before and they'll change the lager keg four or five times before they'll change the Guinness. In a nightclub people can't be bothered to wait for the Guinness to settle.'

'How come you keep the kegs close then and not at the back of the carpark. There's a building out there would work surely? I've seen a couple that are far away from the bar. What's the difference?'

'That building out there is a storeroom. Extra chairs, old tables, think there's an old pool table as well. Wouldn't get too many kegs in. You really want the kegs to be as close to the pumps as possible anyway as a general rule of thumb.'

'Oh yeah?' Remi leaned forward in his chair a little confused. He had to admit he knew very little about bars and keg rooms but he'd assumed they would follow a pattern as much as possible. This was so different to the Marsden's keg room which was in the furthest outbuilding away from the mansion. He mulled it over for a minute.

'You mind if I have a look?' Remi asked seemingly out of nowhere.

'The keg room?' Dylan was surprised. 'Eh, sure. No reason not to. Bob you alright for five?' Bob waved the newspaper he'd started to read after the conversation had turned to keg rooms. He'd no interest in them, only what came from them.

Remi followed Dylan behind the bar and into the back hall of the pub. On the left hand side was an outdoor door. Dylan opened it and sure enough the keg room refrigerated door was within two steps. Dylan opened it and the both went in. Unsure what to show Remi Dylan just let him look for a minute. Remi didn't really know what he was looking for so he settled for small talk.

'Handy the room is here. Saves you a walk!'

'Yeah.' Dylan replied.

'What's the benefit of keeping the pumps close then? Outside of walking time I mean.'

'The further the beer has to travel from the keg the more hassle for the pub. You need more pressure in the gas to get it to travel the distance. The ratio of gas needs adjusting. The lines need to be cleaned more often, then there's a higher chance the beer comes out flat. The general rule of thumb is you want the kegs to be close to the pumps. Cheaper upfront and cheaper maintenance. Beer needs to be cool as well. If you have a cold keg room and long warm pipes you're wasting money.'

Remi shrugged, 'Makes sense now you say it. Thanks man.'

Slowly Tatyana stood and prodded the space in front of her with her toes until she found the carpet rolled up against a wall. On her hands and knees she groped along its edge. Her hands were her guide helping her to figure out which way it had been rolled. When she found the edge at the base it felt dry, she would need to climb over and push from the other side if she was to unroll it but at least signs were good that it wasn't soaked. She straddled the roll and wedged herself between it and the wall before pushing it to unravel. It was heavy, heavier than she thought it would be and she needed to use the wall to lever against. She pushed hard with her arms, at first there was nothing. She pushed again this time the carpet moved slightly and then rocked back. Now it had momentum. Tatyana used that to her advantage. Two more hard pushes and finally it started to roll and took her balance from her. She fell and landed against something hard and cold. And human. Or at least it had been human. Her face fell inches away from Peter's. Even in the darkness of the cell she recognised his scar. Just above the scar his eyes lay staring vacantly past her. Tatyana screamed in terror instantly clambering back away from the lifeless body of the man that had helped rescue her.

The shoebox

It was after ten and Sarah had finally gotten Poppy off to swimming while Giles was outside with the dogs who first needed exercised and then fed. They had both agreed to spend some time alone and think about what next to do before Richard came back later that evening. Recently they hadn't been able to discuss anything without it turning into a shouting match. At least with Richard present there would be a referee and hopefully a better chance of a conversation. In her heart though Sarah was hopeful they'd maybe turned a corner. She had seen in Giles some real concern and tenderness this morning. It had been a long time since she had seen him in this way. Shotgun and ill timed remark aside, his gentleness with Poppy reminded her of the man she had married. At first she thought it had been a show for Richard's benefit, but maybe she was being too harsh on him. They weren't out of the woods but they never would get out if she kept thinking the worst of him.

Her relationship with Giles wasn't the only one that needed rebuilding. She had promised to spend some time with her mother as soon as she could. They were long overdue some kindness to each other. She also needed to bring Tatyana back from the cellar in order to rebuild that relationship. To try and find a better way. Tatyana had pushed her harder than any of the other girls and she wasn't happy with how she was handling the situation. She needed to regain some trust with Tatyana and quickly. A nice hot bath followed by a clean room and freshly made bed went a long way in softening a hardened core. Sarah needed to make amends and she would, starting now, a small gesture but a gesture nonetheless. She had kicked the girls out and told them to watch some TV while she cleaned. After that she wanted a chat with them all about what a new life might look like.

Sarah was in the mood to clean now and decided to do Zusana and Anna's room as well before bringing Tatyana back into the house.

As she stood at the door she wished she hadn't. The room was a mess. Clothes were strewn everywhere making it impossible to identify what was clean and what needed washed. She decided against the sniff test and just picked everything on the floor and threw them into a pile at the door to be washed. Sarah also wanted to strip the beds and have them fresh as well. Anna's bed was clear and easily stripped. Zusana's had a navy wool polo neck jumper and two checked shirts lying on it, all of which were deemed clean. Sarah folded the jumper away in a drawer and went to hang the jumpers in the over crowded wardrobe. Finally she found a hanger that was free hidden in the back and reached to pull it over but couldn't quite grasp it and it fell to the ground and pulling another shirt to the floor at the same time. Sarah cursed and kneeled down to pick up the fallen hanger and shirt. Out of the corner of her eye she saw an old shoebox hidden in the back of the wardrobe floor. It was one of hers from a pair of shoes Giles had first bought her many years ago. She dug past other boxes and handbags and pulled the shoebox out. As she lifted it she shook it. It was light so there wasn't anything in it but she took a mental note to check her wardrobe for the shoes themselves. She threw the box behind her without looking and hung the shirt that had fallen back up.

After she'd hung the shirt and turned back to the room the shoebox she threw had fallen open and the small pieces of paper had fallen out and were scattered across the now clean floor. Sarah sighed and went to pick them up. As she did she looked at them, she knew what these were. Betting slips. Sarah started to sift through the shoebox, it was filled with betting slips. She couldn't believe it. She emptied the box on to the floor. There was so many. At least a hundred. Each slip was worth different amounts, but if they were winning ones they must be worth thousands. Sarah pulled her phone from her pocket and began to add up the amounts. Some slips had a payout amount on them, others didn't so she had to use her limited knowledge of bookie's odds to work out amounts. After half an hour she had totalled the shoe box slips to worth an estimated twelve thousand pounds. She had even googled some of the bigger results, everything bar a couple that she had checked were winners.

Remi sat in the bar unable to finish his pint. He had moved to a table beside a window hoping to evade the thoughts that kept pulling at his conscious. In truth the thoughts were more welcome than his recent ones but still, something wasn't adding up. He couldn't quite grasp it, like a shadow at dusk. He phoned Louise. She didn't answer so he left a voicemail. He explained he was going back for another look at the Marsden's. Something didn't add up and he needed to check it out.

Sarah called the two girls back to their room. She couldn't understand what was going on and needed to get to the bottom of it. Anna and Zusana came in and Sarah showed them the betting slips.

'Whose are these?' Sarah asked, as calmly as possible.

'Ours.' Both girls looked surprised to be asked.

'Where did they come from, are you gambling?' Sarah sat on the edge of the bed and continued before they could answer. 'Girls, I don't want you gambling. Although I must say it looks like you're very good at it. But you can't guarantee it will continue. I know things here aren't what I've wanted for you but I promise I'm working hard to get us a better life.'

'But Mama.' Zusana spoke up. 'We aren't gambling. Mr Giles gives us them.'

'Pardon me?' Sarah couldn't believe what she had just been told. 'Why would Giles give you betting slips?'

'He pays us. Like your friends do.' Zusana spoke matter of factly.

Blood flowed from Sarah's head. She reached her arms out to steady herself from falling.

'Mama, Mama, are you ok?' the young girls went to her and held her arms to help.

A wave of nausea came over Sarah and she had to

hold back her vomit.

Just then Margarite rolled into the bedroom. 'Sarah, sweetheart, can we talk.' She observed the scene in front of her with the betting slips on the floor and Sarah being held and sighed. 'I see you've found out.'

Her mother's words brought the blood back to Sarah's head and snapped Sarah her to the now. 'Found out?' She turned to her mother. 'What do you mean found out? About what? You knew?'

Margarite looked appalled that she was being questioned. 'Yes I knew. And I tried to tell you, but you wouldn't listen to me, You think I don't know what's going on here. In the house of shame.'

'Of course I would listen to you. This. Mum, you never said anything about this.'

'Your marriage is none of my business.' Margarite sat upright in her chair. Justified.

Sarah let out a scream, years of frustration finally finding a channel as she did. 'You're im-fucking-possible mother!' She got up and stormed out of the room. Margarite called after her. 'I tried my best with you. I tried to talk to you but all you ever cared about was this house and keeping up appearances. For a family that never accepted you.'

Sarah stopped and turned to face her mother. 'All I cared about was this house? God you're unbelievable. All I care about is Poppy. The only time you ever seemed happy with anything that I did was when you moved in here. All I've done, everything I've ever done is seeking approval for people who can't give me it. You included. I'm done. I can't do it anymore!' she stormed down the corridor and left Margarite sitting in the hall on her own.

Margarite watched her daughter leave her and softly spoke to her. 'I tried my best.'

Remi made it back to the wall of the Marsden's mansion. He slowly peaked over the stone blocks to take a look. He could see Giles in the courtyard feeding the dogs. Suddenly he regretted coming alone. Just then his phone rang. Loudly. 'Shit!' He dived to the ground behind the wall and scrambled to get the phone on to silent before the ringing alerted Giles or worse, the dogs to his presence.

Remi answered the phone but held his hand over the speaker. He shuffled along to his left where there was a small gap in the stone and he could check and see if he'd been noticed. Giles briefly stopped pouring the dog feed at a noise in the distance but couldn't see anything out of the ordinary and went back to feeding his beloved pets.

Once he was satisfied he was ok Remi spoke 'Lou?' he whispered.

Louise didn't whisper. 'Remi, I swear to god I'm going to kill you. That voicemail you left had better be a joke. Where are you?'

'Lou, calm down. I'm outside the Marsden's. Giles is in the courtyard with the dogs. There's no sign of the kid or Sarah. I'm going to see if I can get a closer look at their keg room. Something is wrong, very wrong Lou.'

'Remi, listen to me. You are dangerously close to losing your job here. You need to back off.'

'I can't do that Lou.' He hung up.

'Shit.' Louise rang back but it went straight to

voicemail.

'That fucking arsehole!'

'Everything alright hun?' Tom looked up from his book. They had been enjoying a rare morning together with the kids at her brother's house and them both off work. Supposedly.

'No. It's Remi he's...'

'It's ok. Go. He needs you. We'll be fine. Just make sure you come home to us.'

'Thanks sweetheart. I'm sorry. We'll reschedule date day?'

Tom smiled and gave her a kiss. 'See you later.'

Louise grabbed the car keys from the kitchen table and left. She was on the phone to Ben and Sam by the time she'd sat in the front seat.

Confrontation

Giles watched the dogs eating from their steel bowls as he drank tea from his thermal mug. He enjoyed the company of dogs. Naturally they made him feel at peace. He was their master. He finished his tea and ruffled the collar of his favourite, Bruno as he decided to get a top up. He'd make Sarah one as well. Another peace offering. Hopefully enough to get her onside for their meeting with Richard later.

Everyone at the law firm had always looked down on him because he wasn't his father. Giles had inherited the account, he inherited his money. He hadn't earned anything he had. Unlike his father who had built upon his father's legacy bringing the Marsden name even more stature. Giles was sure he knew what *they* thought of him. He needed them to see him for who he was. A man in his own right. He would lead the meeting tonight. He would set the agenda. Sarah would support him for once, the head of this household, his household. When she had set up the charity Sarah had chipped away at his authority. She had become the face of the family now leaving him to be viewed as the supporting husband. He was much more than this. He was more than a spoilt child and weak husband. It was time the world knew that he was Giles Marsden.

He let the dogs roam in the courtyard while he went inside to put the kettle on while making a mental note to wear a heavier coat when he took them for their afternoon walk.

Remi watched as Giles left the dogs alone and headed into the house. This was his chance. He skirted around the back of the trees and edged up to the row of outbuildings. After last night he knew the keg room was the building furthest away from the house. This is what didn't make sense to him. If the barman was right then the most sensible and cheapest option was to put the keg room in the building closest to the house. Admittedly he would never understand the thinking of the wealthy but this didn't add up even for them. He decided to start at the keg room and see what he could see. He now had a comparison at least. He stayed at the back of the outbuildings to shield himself from view as he made his way slowly towards the keg room. Only between buildings did he up his pace, barely. Silence not speed was his closest ally. When he got to the third and last outbuilding he tried the door. It was stiff but unlocked. A layer of rust held the door in place. A sharp nudge from his shoulder and it opened clattering as it did. The dogs barked looking around them for the disturbance. Giles however knocked the kitchen window shutting them up.

Sarah sat on her bed in her bedroom, in tears. Her life had been pulled apart. She felt so foolish. She had risked everything for Giles. For his family. To keep hold of the things that he had been given. She had done unspeakable things. She had asked the girls to do unspeakable things, for her family. And he had just played her for a fool. Anger grew inside her.

Remi looked around the keg room. Although he had seen the room in the bar he still wasn't sure what it was that he was looking for. So he started moving kegs around. Hoping something would jump out at him. Something tangible.

Tatyana sat in the cell. Her tears had dried up and she had wiped the vomit from her mouth. She couldn't take her eyes off Peter's lifeless body. No matter how hard she tried she could only look at his face, his eyes fixed staring beyond her yet piercing her at the same time. She knew she needed to get out of there otherwise she'd be next. Then she heard it. Next door. Someone was there. She went over to the wall to listen carefully stepping over Peter's body. Her hand cupped her ear as she leaned against the stone wall hoping to hear a clue as to who it was.

She listened, her body motionless as she did. All she heard was silence. She waited. Still nothing. She pulled back but as she did she heard it again. Faintly. A scraping. She couldn't picture what it was. She heard it again. As if someone was moving something heavy across the floor. This was her chance. She hit the wall with her hands and screamed as loudly as she could. She had decided if she was going to die, it wouldn't be quietly.

Next door Remi was moving the kegs from one side to another with no luck. Nothing was making any sense. He sat down on one of the kegs to think. To look. He scanned the room but nothing stood out. Finally it hit him, he'd made a mistake. There was nothing. His grief was clouding his judgement. He shouldn't be here. He'd pissed Lou off, he'd let the team down and he was risking everything he had left to...to what? He didn't even know anymore. Exhausted he sat in the cold of the keg room alone.

Then he heard something. He froze. He heard it again, the faintest of cries invading the silence of the keg room. He stood up and listened harder. He followed the noise. It was coming from behind him. Remi thought. This was the last of the outbuildings. There was nothing on the other side of this. It must be a fake wall. He looked around but there was no sign of it. He pulled the three kegs that were tapped into the pumps away from the wall. That's when he saw it. Behind the third keg at the very corner. A change in the light betraying the slightest of gaps. He knelt down and felt the edge with his fingers. Strangely there wasn't any breeze despite the wind outside. His eyes searched the wall for more clues but he couldn't see any. He pushed the wall. It moved, barely, but it moved. He pushed some more. He had found it, a false wall with a door. The pumps that the kegs were attached to hid the frame from sight. He pulled the door back. The screams were louder now. There was a large metal door with a lever handle in front of him.

Adrenaline pumping through him Remi called out. 'Hello?' No answer. He called louder this time. 'Anyone there?'

He'd made a mistake. Outside the dogs heard and started to bark for the second time. Giles was pouring tea for him and Sarah in the kitchen when he heard the dogs barking. He raised his hand to bang the window but stopped short. Something was wrong. He put his cup down and went outside to see what was happening. As he got to the courtyard the dogs were standing barking outside the keg room. They must have found something.

Remi pulled back the door to see what was behind it. The punch came out of the darkness and he didn't have a chance to see it. Tatyana hit him in the face. Her punch surprised him more than hurt him but it did enough for her to try and squeeze past him. Remi grabbed her by the waist to stop her as she squirmed to get out of his grasp.

Remi pulled his other arm around her and held her in a bear hug to calm her. 'I'm the police, I'm here to help.'

'I don't think your warrant stretched this far officer!' Remi turned behind him to see Giles standing in the keg room with his three dogs snarling at his side.

Instinctively Remi put his body between Tatyana and Giles. He went to pull his gun but grabbed air, he didn't carry when wearing civilian clothes. As a policeman he was naked. That didn't matter. He now had Giles. He couldn't get out of this.

'Giles Marsden, I'm arresting you...' He didn't get to finish his sentence.

'Get him!' Giles commanded the dogs. All three dogs charged at Remi and attacked his legs. He tried to move back but it was too late. The dogs were on him immediately. Remi kicked at them. He got lucky and connected with the first dogs jaw. It broke it and the dog lay down on the ground incapacitated. The other two were harder. The larger of the two remaining dogs jumped and bit his right forearm, Remi cried out in pain. He swung wildly trying to get the dog off but it had clamped hard. Its teeth sinking through Remi's jacket and into his skin. The third dog was snapping at his heels and Remi had to thrash his legs around to keep it at bay. Remi was scrambling. He was fighting to stay upright. If he ended up on the ground the dogs would have him. His childhood fears were beginning to choke him from the inside and he became weaker. Giles used the distraction to grab Tatyana by the hair and pull her to him.

But Tatyana sensed freedom in the air, she would not let it go. She kicked Giles hard in the shin. The sharp pain made him let go of her. Tatyana tried to push her way past. She squeezed into a gap between him and the wall elbowing Giles in the side as she did so. This made him see red and he grabbed her hair pulling her back and threw her against the kegs. She let out a moan as her back cracked against the cold steel.

Remi had lost his battle to stay on his feet. The two dogs had worn him down and he was now bleeding on the ground protecting his face as they mauled at him. Assessing that Remi was the greater threat Giles stood over him and pulled out a hunting knife from his pocket.

'Time for you to spend some time with your wife!'

The gunshot echoed in the keg room. The dogs yelped and ran for cover. Giles' body arched forward and fell on top of Remi who pushed him away to see Sarah standing at the doorway of the keg room with the shotgun in her hand. They both looked at each other and said nothing. After a moment of silence Sarah threw the gun on the ground and went over to Tatyana. She helped the young girl up and draped her arm over her shoulder. 'Let's get you cleaned up sweetheart.'

Tatyana turned to Remi. He wasn't sure if she spoke the words or mouthed them because he couldn't hear above the ringing in his ears, either way he needed help because it looked as though she said 'Help me'. Remi nodded. Sarah said nothing as she led Tatyana out of the keg room and into the courtyard. It was only when she reached the door did she turn. The ringing subsiding enough for him to hear the words 'I'm sorry for what my husband did to your family.'

In the distance Remi heard police sirens and he put his head back on the ground to rest. His body ached, his face was bleeding. His grief decided it was time to talk. When his tears came they didn't stop.

Outside Sarah sat beside Tatyana who was still shaking from fear. Sarah held her tightly, her arm around her. Tatyana resisted and tried break free from the grip of the monster. Sarah spoke as she tightened her grip on her keeping her in place.

'You have about two minutes to decide where your life goes. I know you don't want to listen to me now but I'm going to tell you what's about to happen. The police are coming and they are going to ask you what happened. What you tell them is up to you. What happens however is not. You can tell them I put you in the cell and I'll go to jail. They will then put you on the first plane back to that shithole I found you in. I'm sure your brothers will have missed you.' Sarah could feel Tatyana stiffen at the prospect. She continued. 'There is however option B. You won't like it, and you'll have to trust me. I understand that part will be hard for you. But if you do you'll benefit. Giles put you in the cell. I didn't know anything about it. They'll believe you. If you do this, you'll get your freedom and I'll give you a house. Same as Anna and Zusana. One each. You'll never see me again.' Tatyana didn't say anything in response. Police swarmed into the courtyard and an officer took her to be examined. She looked back once as she was led away.

Months Later

Sarah let her fingers linger for just a moment on each book as she browsed through the personal library of Theodore Reinholdt. She had never been a big reader but as she stood and inhaled the opulence of the judge's study she finally understood the appeal. The knowledge one person could gain just from this room alone was immense. Knowledge that could be honed and turned to power. Volumes upon volumes of wisdom and understanding from throughout history were at her fingertips. The internet had this, but not in this way. It wasn't tangible. In here you could hold it, smell it, feel it.

Her eyes stopped, drawn to a title. Slowly she pulled it from the shelf, drawn by its spell. 'The 48 Laws of Power' by Robert Greene. She opened the cover and began to read.

Engrossed in the text she didn't hear Theodore Reinholdt come in.

'Sarah, my dear, what a pleasant surprise.' Six months had passed since they had last seen each other. Nervous about how they had ended Sarah had requested the meeting. She spun round as though she'd been caught reading her sister's diary. She slammed the book shut and went to put it back on the shelf. 'Sorry, I shouldn't…'

'Never apologise for wanting to learn. It is man's greatest trait. Let me see.' Reinholdt came closer and took the book from her hand. Dressed in beige slacks, a pinstriped shirt with the top two buttons loosened, and a navy jacket that tried its best to contain his heavy frame the Judge was clearly relaxed after a long days work. A wry smile came across his lips as he saw the cover. She smelt the mix of cognac and cigar on his breath as he spoke.

'A personal favourite of mine. You may keep it. As a gift.' He handed it back. 'Please take a seat, I must say I was surprised to get your call.' He indicated to a soft armchair for Sarah as he eased his frame into what was clearly his favoured chair. The indentations moulded around him as he did so.

Sarah was unsure if she'd made the right call in meeting him but she didn't want the dread of reprisals hanging over her now. She needed to see where this went. His demeanour was pleasant but she knew that didn't mean anything with him.

'I like what you've done with your hair. It suits you.' Reinholdt was comfortable here. He had an ease about him that was almost seductive. Sarah could feel the power emanating from him and was drawn to him. She pushed the hair on her left side behind her ear. She'd cut her hair after Giles's funeral. Her way of cutting herself from her past. It was sharper, more severe around her face but combined with a little dye and it took years from her. In truth it wasn't just the haircut. She was sleeping better now.

All the finances of the Marsden family had

transferred to Sarah after Giles's death. She had been cleared of any charges after Remi was able to confirm her story that Giles was about to kill him. Tatyana and the girls held their stories. The police had been able to trace the betting slips back to Giles which only confirmed the stories. She was able to shed the remainder of Giles's investment properties for only a small loss and the mansion had sold relatively quickly, a bargain for the buyer but enough for Sarah and Poppy to downscale, clear all the family debts and have enough left over to put Margarite in a home. As a thank you for holding up their end of the bargain all three girls were now living in modest houses mortgage free paid for by Sarah. Their freedom guaranteed. Although she didn't speak with Tatyana at all she had regular visits from Zusana and Anna. The one item from the Marsden dynasty that Sarah didn't sell was the necklace. She had kept that for when Poppy was older.

Her new found financial freedom had given her a new lease of life. The knot in her stomach she had carried for years while married to Giles and his family legacy no longer visited her. The pressure that had bore down on her for so long was now removed. She now had the time and space to reclaim herself. To focus on her motivations and what was important to her. She was here to work on those very things.

Inside her left hand jacket pocket she kept her insurance. She had found the letter Peter's sister had written all those years ago in the pocket of his combat trousers as she said goodbye to his body. When no-one was looking she had stuffed it in her bra. She had read it that night as she sat alone in the empty mansion and the seeds of her plan began to germinate over the next few days.

'I'm sure you've heard about my circumstances since we last spoke?' Her voice remained calm.

'Terrible business all that. My condolences about Giles. He'll be missed.'

'Not by me. He was useless, in every single way.'

Reinholdt snorted in agreement. 'Quite.' After a moments silence his smile quickly dropped. 'What brings you to my house Sarah?'

She composed herself. 'You're a man of discerning tastes Teddy. We both know that. We also both know the prostitutes you're visiting don't live up to your requirements.' She inspected her nails almost absentmindedly as she spoke. Playing a character she had rehearsed.

'My wife is next door. I suggest you keep your voice down or leave'. Reinholdt shifted nervously in his chair.

Sarah continued unabated. She had buried her naivety alongside Giles as well as any deference she had previously given men like Reinholdt. She was in control now.

'Your exact requirements. I'm guessing there is a desire you have inside you that hasn't been met in some long months.' She let the words hang in the air as she probed his face for clues to his thinking. He gave no response so she continued.

'I thought that I might be able to help you...to enable you to satisfy those desires. I man like yourself clearly is used to the finer things in life. I suggest you shouldn't be deprived of anything this life has to offer.'

Reinholdt sat back in his chair, eyebrows raised. 'From what I gathered, you had finished. A change of heart was the rumour. Or perhaps a crisis of conscience is more apt? In addition your charity no longer exists. I'm not so sure you're in a position to offer such a service.'

She had him. She knew it. The tension she felt ten minutes ago had been replaced by excitement coursing through her blood. She began to feel alive again.

'I would be hesitant about making inferences with incomplete information.'

'Do pray tell'

'Let me put it this way, when you lose everything it focusses the mind on what is important to you. The last few months I've been able think without the distraction of looking after Giles. As it turns out, I like being in power and control. Life is extremely boring when you're reduced to just doing the school run. Obviously without the charity in place I've had to adapt my business model. I've learnt and grown, found alternative routes. All of which has been of benefit. The product, my product it's even better.'

Reinholdt smiled. 'I always liked you Sarah. You'll join me in a toast?' He rose from his chair and went to the drinks cabinet in the corner of the study and poured two glasses of Louis XIII cognac into crystal glasses.

'To new beginnings.'

'New beginnings.'

She wouldn't need to use the letter today after all. She would keep it for another day should the need arise. Reinholdt was a horrible man who did not forget even the smallest of slights easily.

The chink of the crystal echoed in the air as they both drank to a new era. Their eyes locked above the rim of the glasses. Their uneasy arrangement had been agreed both knowing a relationship built on a fracture could not last.

Sarah smiled as therein lied the appeal.

ABOUT THE AUTHOR

Paul Scott lives on the shores of Strangford Lough in Northern Ireland with his wife and two children. To Protect is his first novel.

When not shouting at his computer screen he can be found enjoying the water or mountains and has been known to eat a full packet of chocolate hob nobs in one sitting.

Printed in Great Britain
by Amazon

45609329R00136